Sabotage

Kevin Moran

www.aninkmover.com

For my beautiful bride

1

Stad watched the bomb on the passenger seat slide around as the old truck rattled through the residential street. He took his foot off the gas to let the speedometer drop below 25 and made sure the unassuming package settled on the cracked leather. He turned right onto Baltimore and followed the path engraved in his memory.

He straightened the wheel and a drop of sweat dripped down from his forehead, glanced off his nose and landed in his lap. It wasn't hot outside, but the stress and explosives made it feel like it was pushing one hundred. He reached over and manually rolled down the window to let in the cool Seattle air. The truck was aged and beat up, but for the limited use he needed it for, it was reliable enough. The salesman was eager to get rid of it and Stad had an easy time talking him down, and it only got easier when he started pulling out hundred-dollar bills.

Stad turned onto Wentwood and checked the package again. When he was comfortable knowing that the bomb wasn't going anywhere, his attention turned to the houses passing by. He drove past cookie-cutter homes with big trees in the front yard and two-car garages and he remembered every detail. All the houses looked like a perfect family setting but he knew the dark, forgotten corners of their garages were cluttered with crap. Block after block the houses repeated themselves until Stad passed another intersection and the garages got a little bigger, the windows got a little brighter and the lawns got a lot more attention.

3564 South Wentwood was on the right side and waiting just a couple of blocks down. Stad brought the truck to a crawl and stopped a few feet away from their mailbox. It was a good sized colonial that had four or five bedrooms, an office or a home theater in the basement, a couple of dining rooms and a nice deck in the back.

Stad checked himself out in the rear-view mirror to make sure his sunglasses and hat covered most of his face and to see if there were prying eyes in the area. He picked up the bomb, which seemed to have gained fifty pounds during the long drive, and stepped out of his running truck. He walked over to the mailbox, pulled the lid down and squeezed the package inside. He eased it in, but with every new scratch came another bead of sweat rolling down his face. He took a deep breath and shoved the last inch of the package inside, wiped the sweat from his head and closed the lid. He trotted back over to his waiting truck and drove off.

Further down the road he did another quick check in his mirrors for signs of life and found none. He pulled off onto a side street and stopped underneath a large oak tree. He reached into his glove compartment and pulled out a simple, gray, two-buttoned device that anyone else would mistake for a garage door opener. He pushed the button when 1:29 disappeared into 1:30. Staring into his mirror he watched the horizon in the distance. The peaceful autumn sky was shattered by an explosion and a billowing puff of smoke. Stad pulled out from underneath the shade and wiped away another drop of sweat that had found its way to his eyebrows.

2

Stad parked in the giant lot of the closest Supercenter, made sure there was nothing in or on the car that could be tracked to him and headed for the entrance. The automatic doors slid open and he was greeted with an overpowering fluorescent glow, the smell of plastic and an endless row of registers, two of which were operational.

He trekked across the linoleum until he almost ran over an old woman hiding behind a clothes rack. She looked up in her employee-standard blue polo shirt and caught Stad's eyes.

Shit.

Stad snapped his head in the other direction and looked away from the sad, saggy and depressed face staring back. He carried on his own way and she went back to rummaging through the dresses on the rack without saying anything. He was flustered from the contact but got back on track by locating the banner that said "Hair Care." He composed himself and headed in that direction. He passed one aisle that contained a bunch of who cares, followed by another where the shelves were stocked full of crap nobody needs. He turned a corner and his shoes squeaked against the polished floor, sending an alert to another blue shirted employee nearby. The man headed for Stad and his wrinkled face turned from pure boredom to enlightenment.

"Can I help you sir?"

No, absolutely not, not a chance in hell.

All the things Stad wanted to say ran through his head, but all that came out was a lousy "No" and he kept moving his legs in the direction of the hair products tucked away in the back corner.

He picked up his pace to escape any follow-up questions and when he reached the far corner of the store he headed down an aisle where a lady with oversized glasses resting on top of her head was staring at curling irons. He stopped mid stride and pretend to be interested in hair coloring kits. From his peripheral he could see another employee standing next to her and he could hear words being thrown around like "non-slip grip" and "25 temperature controls" and "dual voltage." Uninterested in the topic, he forced himself to keep listening. After more buzzwords and industry lingo were thrown around the employee mentioned something about credit cards and he and the woman took one of the curling irons from the shelf and left. If they had stayed any longer, Stad would have either killed himself out of boredom or given his hair a splash of golden highlights.

Now alone, he shuffled over to the blow dryers and examined each one, making close observations of the warning labels strangling the electric cords. It didn't take long for him to find what he was looking for. On one of the tags in big white letters were the words "DO NOT USE IN SHOWER." He pulled a black marker from his back pocket and created a near perfect rectangle across the letters and blended them in with the dark background. He took a step back to admire his work and decided that any customer in a hurry wouldn't see the cover-up job. He went down the line and repeated the procedure to the three other blow dryers on the shelf. After he was done and satisfied he capped the marker and made his way to the exit. On the way out he reached for his phone and dialed the number for the local taxi company. Once outside of the mega store he found a spot near the entrance with a nice breeze and waited for the cab to arrive.

3

"Wait here." Stad handed the driver a fifty and stepped out of the cab. The hotel was below average and although he preferred better conditions, he cared more about keeping his low profile. He passed through the unfamiliar front doors and the smell of chlorine caught him off guard and smacked him in the face. He forced himself to ignore it and breezed by the woman at the reception desk without as much as a nod in her direction.

His room was in the middle of a long hallway of doors, even though he had requested one on the end. It wasn't worth it to him to have to interact with anyone to get it changed, so he lived with it. The room was hotel standard with a king bed underneath a piece of amateur art, an oversized lounger next to the window, a decent TV and a Bible in the drawer next to the phone book. Over his three-day occupancy Stad had added his own flairs, including his clothes from last night scattered around the room. He had met up with a woman at the lobby bar who was going on and on about the conference she was here for, or something, he wasn't really listening anyway. He had the right mix of buying drinks, nodding along and funny comments to end up with her in his bed at the end of the night.

"I've got this really important session this morning and I can't miss it." Stad's mind wandered off to her screeching voice this morning. He was propped up against the headboard, shirtless and hung over and was watching her scurry around the room trying to collect her things.

"I can't be late. Have you seen my pants? I can't find my pants." She got on her hands and knees to examine the space beneath the bed. Stad yawned.

"Seriously, my boss will kill me if I miss this." She turned her attention to the area beneath the lounger and Stad looked out the window.

"It was the *one* mandatory meeting, of course." She threw the pillows off the lounger and squeezed her hands between the cushions. Stad scratched his stubble.

"Do you think my car is still okay in the parking lot? I hope they didn't tow it or anything." She headed for the bathroom. "Seriously, where are my pants?" Stad could hear the shower curtain sliding around. He closed his eyes and fell back asleep. He didn't notice when she got around to finding her pants and leaving.

He collected his scattered clothes, grabbed his money from the safe, his toothbrush from the bathroom counter and stuffed it all in his small duffel bag. He left his keycard by the TV, the sheets a mess, threw the "Do Not Disturb" sign onto the floor and made sure the door closed behind him.

The taxi took him to the airport where he printed out his boarding pass, waddled through the security line and waited by the gate.

He couldn't believe his jobs were getting this easy. A few materials here, some rough planning ahead of time and soon enough he'd be getting paid all over again. One of the TVs above him was changed to the local news and the top story caught his attention. It was about a local bombing in the suburbs. He held back an oncoming grin.

4

The flight landed ahead of schedule at the Dallas airport and Stad couldn't get off the plane fast enough, trying to escape the crowd of people lugging around their oversized suitcases and whiny kids. He hopped into another cab that took him to another hotel. He dropped his duffel bag at his feet and rang the bell that sat at the reception counter.

"Hi." A twenty-something, perky girl appeared from somewhere in the back.

"Yeah I'm checking in. Patrick Smith."

"What brings you to Dallas today, Mr. Smith?"

"It should be a king bed."

"I'll double check for you." Her smile faded and Stad looked out the glass door and picked at his teeth. After a few moments of tooth picking and keys clacking the receptionist handed over a plastic keycard.

"Your room is 218, second floor, down the hall, to the left."

"Thanks." Stad picked up his bag and shuffled toward the hallway. The layout was similar to his last room with yet another chair, another bed and another crappy piece of art. He tossed his bag on the floor and checked the clock. If he hurried, he could still make happy hour.

There was a bar across the street called "Howlers" and it seemed as good a place as any. It was full of loose ties, loose women and loose wallets. He found an open stool at the end of the bar.

"What can I get for you?" A man who didn't look old enough to be serving alcohol set his hands on the bar and leaned over.

"Scotch and seven."

"You got a tab?"

"Is this enough?" Stad threw a couple of twenties down and counted on it to cover the tip and keep the drinks flowing for the night.

"Yeah, that should be fine." The young bartender started reaching for the required bottles. "What brings you in here tonight?"

Damn. Too much tip.

"Business trip."

"Ah come on, that's everyone's story, I was hoping you'd have something more exciting."

If only he knew maybe he wouldn't be saying the same thing.

"Sorry, that's the best I got for you."

"Well at least tell me what you're here for, what do you do?"

"I'm an accountant."

"You work around here or…?"

"Client called up last minute, wanted to go over some finances."

"How'd it go?" The bartender set the drink down in front of Stad.

"Don't know, flew in this afternoon." The scotch was strong.

"Well then when is it?"

"Tomorrow."

"So you'll be sticking around here for a while then?" He started wiping down non-existent spills on the counter.

"No." Stad took another drink. "Staying just long enough to have some drinks on the company dollar."

"In that case, just let me know when you need that refilled." The bartender left and Stad started eyeing the women around him. There were plenty, but he had a self-imposed rule to never make the first move. Sometimes he broke it, but tonight he didn't have to. He was several drinks in when three young women took the stools next to his.

"You can put that on my tab if you want." The bartender had just mixed up three drinks and set them down when Stad turned in his seat to the brunette closest to him.

"What?" she asked.

"You can put that on my tab if you want."

"You sure?"

"Yeah, it's just money."

The brunette held up one finger and huddled with her friends. Stad just looked straight ahead and took a longer-than-usual drink from his glass.

"Okay, thanks."

He was in.

"No problem, my name's Stad."

"I'm Jaime, this is Tiffany and Morgan."

"Hey, nice to meet you all." He was close enough to Jaime to shake her hand but had to wave to her other friends whose names he had already forgotten.

Over even more drinks he listened to them but didn't process any of the words. When asked about himself he'd just say the bare minimum. None of them knew anything about accounting but even if they had he was sure he could fake it to get by. It was easy to pass the conversational puck to them and keep them talking.

"We'll take another round." Stad threw some more money down and the bartender was quick to return with the drinks.

"Thanks, Stad," Jaime said. Her friends had formed their own conversation and were talking about the latest celebrity gossip. "You know, I really wish more guys were like you." She inched closer to his over-the-limit breathe. "You're just so easy to talk to, not like some of the other jerks who only care about themselves."

"Yeah," he muttered. "Jerks."

"We're going to the bathroom." The friend furthest away leaned forward to catch Jaime's attention. "You coming?"

"No, I'm okay," Jaime said. Her comment was shrugged off and the two friends left Jaime alone with Stad.

"You really get along with them?" Stad asked when the friends were out of earshot.

"I used to a lot better. The two of them have always been closest friends, even when I was around. It's especially harder now that we all live in different spots. I feel like they don't care a whole lot. I felt like the third wheel sometimes in college, but now it's just worse, you know?"

"Tell me about it."

"Hey." She leaned in even closer. "You want to get out of here?"

"Yeah, I mean, I'm right across the street. Is that cool with your friends?"

"I'm sure they won't mind, I didn't come here with them or anything. I should let them know though, I'll be back." She headed off to follow her friends and Stad made quick work of the rest of his drink. Jaime reappeared after a few minutes.

"Ready?" she asked.

The two made their way for the front and Jaime looked up and smiled at Stad. He half-smiled back and followed her through the door and out into the night.

5

Stad rolled over and ran into an unexpected pile of hair. He pulled his head back and wiped his mouth of random strands that were left behind. It took him a few seconds to realize it was the girl from last night, but he couldn't remember her name. Jen, Jesse, Jaime? Jaime sounded right. He stared at her for a few moments, sleeping on her side and breathing into the pillow.

He edged his way to the side of the bed and slipped out of the sheets. He crept away from the undisturbed, sleeping heap of sheets and set his sights on the coffee pot. He popped off the top, threw in one of the crappy filters the hotel provided, added some water, turned it on and watched it come to life. He splashed his face with cold water and checked himself out in the mirror. His eyes were almost pure red, his hair was smashed to his skull and a grid of lines had formed across his cheek. He rubbed his hands against his face trying to get rid of the lines but gave up when he didn't make any progress. He shuffled over to the window and cracked open the shade to the view of the back of another building and a homeless man sleeping against a brick wall.

"Good morning."

He turned around and saw Jaime leaning against the headboard. "Hey." It was all that he could think to say.

"Coffee maker woke me up."

"Oh yeah, sorry."

"No, it's all right, I need to get going anyway." She jumped up out of bed in nothing but her underwear, gathered her clothes and headed for the bathroom. As she got ready, Stad unwrapped the plastic cups and poured himself some coffee. He headed back to the window and opened the shades all the way. He sipped his coffee and tried to figure out if the homeless man was sleeping or dead.

"How's the coffee?" Jaime emerged from the bathroom in the same clothes she was wearing last night. Stad thought they were as flattering now as they had been six hours ago.

"Not terrible."

She picked up her purse from the TV stand. "I'm going to go now." She stood there, purse in one hand and the other one resting on her hip.

"Okay."

"I guess I'll see you around?"

"Probably only when I'm in town."

"Are you going to be around any longer this week?"

"No, I'm leaving tonight." Stad took a sip of his coffee.

"Well how often are you here?"

"Not very."

"I should give you my number just in case." She grabbed a pen and a wrapper of some kind from her purse. She scribbled a few numbers down and handed it over. "Here. Don't lose it."

"Oh I won't." Stad waited until he heard the door close before tossing it in the trash.

6

After 35 dollars worth of driving, the taxi pulled up to a dinky building in the center of a massive lot full of cars old and new. When Stad stepped out two men rushed from inside and scurried to his side.

"Hello sir, how can we help you?" The man with his sleeves rolled up past his elbows was talking while the other man in the purple tinged suit was nodding along.

"I'm looking to buy a small four-door. Something simple."

"Won't be a problem here, we got plenty to choose from. I'm Bob Carrie and this is my associate, Martin. We'll help you find what you need. We've got some great deals that just came in if you're interested."

"I don't have much time this morning and I have this wad of cash." He pulled out a wet clump of bills from his back pocket. "So let's say we work out a deal now and everyone gets on their way?"

"Whatever works for you. How about that red one over there?" Bob looked over his shoulder and pointed at a car in the distance.

"What's the mileage?"

"Martin, check the mileage on that one."

"And the condition?"

"Oh it's good, that's all we carry here at Carrie's." Bob Carrie chuckled at his own joke.

"Does the air work?"

"Martin," Bob called out to his partner who was halfway to the car, "check the air too." He faced Stad again and hooked his hands into his front pockets, almost out of breathe just from shouting. "Can I ask what brings you out looking for a car today?"

"I just need one."

"No problem, as soon as my associate confirms everything's in good condition we can write you up and get you on your way." Bob watched his partner circle around the car and Stad kicked the dirt. Martin gave his boss two thumbs up and Bob opened his mouth again. "Looks like it's in excellent condition, everything works and the mileage is under a hundred grand."

"You got all of that from two thumbs?"

"Martin and I can practically read each others' minds."

"Whatever." Stad shrugged. "Where do I sign?"

"If you'll just follow me inside I can write up the deal for you." Bob started toward the building and Stad followed. "How much you got in that stack anyway?"

"How much of it do you want for the car?"

"I'll wait for Martin to meet up with us and we can work out something. It'll be a heck of a deal, promise." Bob chuckled again and the bell above clinked against the glass door. Stad kept throwing hundreds on the table until the two salesmen were satisfied and after signing the last line they shook Stad's hand and tossed him the keys. Stad wandered back out across the dirt lot, started the car up and pulled out, leaving Bob and Martin behind to try and woo the next customers.

7

The targets weren't picked out at random, but there wasn't a lengthy screening process either. Multiple statistics and cross reference reports were checked well in advance. In this particular neighborhood there were manicured lawns and pruned trees lined up and waiting for the next car to parade down the street. The only difference between houses, other than the paint, was whether or not the flag on the mailbox was up or down. Stad drove past a fountain in the median and was careful not to exceed the posted limit of 25.

498 Ford Drive was just like the other houses on the street. The lawn was clipped with thought, the driveway had new pavement, the paint showed no signs of peeling and the windows were crystal clean with unnecessary exterior shutters. The backyard was empty except for a hammock between two tall trees. All of the blinds for the windows on the front of the house were half closed but when he looked at just the right angle he could see inside. There weren't any signs of anyone home and he didn't notice the telltale signs of a pet, any lawn or cleaning services and nothing that would indicate a child lived there. His research had already told him all of this information, but he always had to double check once he arrived on site.

At the next intersection he took a left and parked on the side of the street. His car was facing away from his target but he could still see it in his rear and side mirrors. He tilted his hat forward and pretended to nap. Activity in the area was close to none, so he wasn't too worried about anyone noticing. Watching the house through his mirrors, he staked the place out.

The activity level was lower than he thought it would be and he let his mind wander. He kept going back to the bar and wondered what the mix would be like tonight. Last night wasn't too bad but he preferred more of a challenge. Jaime was a heck of a lay though, near the top in his recent memory at least. He knew that after a while she would just start to blur together with all the others.

Nothing happened until 3:00 when kids started to pop up out of nowhere. Stad hadn't expected it but he wasn't surprised either. His research showed this neighborhood to be mostly young, childless couples but he knew that his reports had been somewhat inaccurate before.

At 4:30 the mail truck hovered around the target's mailbox for close to 30 seconds before pulling up to the next house.

At 4:52 a black sedan pulled into the garage.

At 4:55 a bearded man that Stad knew as Adam Wesley dragged two trash cans to the curb and returned to the garage to bring out a recycling bin. He dropped off the bins and stopped at the mailbox to collect the mail. After marching to and from the curb, the man disappeared into the house and the garage door shut behind him. A lamp turned on in the living room and when flickering lights were quick to follow, Stad pictured Mr. Wesley sitting on the couch enjoying sports highlights before his wife got home.

At 5:40 a silver coupe parked in the driveway. The flickering lights of the TV stopped when the car did and the kitchen lights came to life. Mrs. Wesley stepped out of the car and walked through the front door.

At 6:20 the Wesleys emerged, entered the silver car with Mr. Wesley in the driver's seat and headed north. Stad waited until 6:30 to be sure they wouldn't be coming back for a forgotten item before pulling his hat up and out of his face and starting the engine.

8

The traffic was thinned out by the time Stad reached the interstate and it didn't take him long to reach the familiar airport. The lines at the ticket booth were short as most people used the automatic machines to check in and get any information, but because Stad had a strict cash-only policy he had to approach the overweight woman standing behind the counter.

"Can I help you?" she asked with a slight southern drawl. Her oversized hair moved with the beat of the syllables.

"I'm looking for a flight to Indianapolis on the 15th."

"Two days from now, that's short notice."

"What's available in the early afternoon?" Stad listened to her hammer away at the keyboard in front of her.

"We have flights leaving at 1:47 and one at 4:05. There are also flights leaving throughout the evening."

"I'll take the 1:47 flight."

"Will you be carrying any bags on board with us?" She looked up and had a goofy smile slathered across her face.

"Just my carry-on."

"And are you traveling with any pets or children?"

"No."

"Are you a member of our rewards program?"

"No."

"Would you like to be? It'll only take a minute to fill out."

"No, just the ticket."

"Not a problem, just give me a few minutes here. I'll also need to see your ID and credit card you'll be paying with."

"Is cash all right?" Stad threw his fake ID onto the counter.

"Cash is more than all right, Mr. ... Smith." She looked up and had the same smile on her face. "Just a few more minutes here and you'll be all set." Stad listened to her type a novel before everything was ready. "The total cost for your flight to Indianapolis on the 15th is going to be $413.27 with tax." Her southern accent couldn't be mistaken when she said "tax." Stad laid down five hundred-dollar bills on the counter, waited for his ticket to be printed and managed to escape without one "ya'll" being uttered from behind the desk. He couldn't wait to get back to the bar.

***

"You liked it so much you couldn't stay away, huh?" The bartender from last night was quick to meet Stad. "Sticking with the scotch and seven?"

"For now."

"Sure. I mean it treated you so well last night, why would you want to change it up?"

"What?"

"I'm just saying that girl you took home last night was pretty attractive. Wish I could pull something like that."

"Oh, yeah." Stad turned his head to check out the rest of the place and although it wasn't as busy as last night, it still had a sizeable crowd.

"Who are you aiming for tonight?"

"I don't really do that, it just sort of happens, you know?"

"No, actually. Most of us don't know."

Stad shrugged.

"Enjoy the drink." The bartender placed Stad's glass on the counter and walked away. Stad counted three more drinks before a woman wound up in the barstool next to his.

"You got a light?" she asked.

"You know you really shouldn't smoke."

"Who are you, the surgeon general?"

"I can be if you want me to be." After chatting and finding out she was a divorcée whose new boyfriend stood her up for their two week anniversary he realized this would be easier than he thought. He would say it was like shooting fish in a barrel, but it would probably be more accurate to say it was like shooting boots in a barrel with a shotgun.

He forgot her name somewhere along the way but kept paying for drinks and nodding along. He soon found himself ordering just for one as she couldn't keep up with him.

"Hey, listen." Stad leaned over during a moment of silence. "I'm staying across the street if you want to head out." He leaned back and waited for a response.

"Sure," she said.

Before escorting her out, Stad slapped down some money on the counter as more of a show than anything.

9

The next day Stad parked on an adjacent side street facing the target house. It was a little colder and early in the morning around 9:00 a couple of city workers showed up in their green trucks to turn off the fountain. They were slow and lazy and Stad figured it took them an hour longer than it should have to finish the job, which they got around to doing by 11:00.

The same pattern played out as the day before once the city workers left the picture. He thought about that woman from the bar last night and tried to remember her name. It didn't matter to him but he liked the challenge. The name Kristen kept coming to his mind but he was pretty sure he was thinking of a woman he met in Boston last year.

Kids started showing up at 3:00 and were out of sight by 4:00. Mr. Wesley arrived home early around 4:25 and Stad saw him trot out to the mailbox only to be frustrated when nothing was inside. The man double checked to make sure the mail wasn't shoved all the way in the back, but when none was discovered he slammed the tiny door and walked back to the house. Three minutes later the mail truck showed up. Before it could make its way to the next home, Mr. Wesley had opened the front door and was halfway down the driveway. He gave a slight wave to the mailman before the truck was out of sight. He grabbed what looked like a stack of envelopes and one large mailer which Stad figured was full of useless coupons.

Mr. Wesley's wife got home at 6:00 and only spent a few moments in the house before reappearing with her husband and getting in the silver coupe, which they used to head north again. Stad checked his watch, waited five more minutes and then pulled out into the street.

10

Stad's supplier was random with his drop off points and today Stad found himself picking up the contents at a local P.O. box. He walked in to a crowded building with people snaking through a line to mail their packages and buy the latest collector stamps. Stad kept walking and hoped that he could remain invisible. The key for the box had been mailed to him weeks ago and it worked as expected when he turned it in the lock.

Inside was a familiar brown paper package that looked like either a small, plain gift or a hunk of meat. Stad had to tug at it to get it out of the tight-fitting slot. After freeing it he checked it over a few times for damage or wear and tear that could compromise his safety or the job in any way. It had a few scratches that Stad had become accustomed to dealing with but they were nothing major. He closed and locked the box, tucked the package under his arm and headed back for his car.

He followed the same path that he had taken the past couple of days until he wound up in front of the familiar house. He stopped on the side of the road about ten feet behind the mailbox, kept his car running and stepped outside. When he reached the mailbox he opened it and found nothing inside, just like the little flag indicated, so he eased the package in and slid it toward the back. When he was satisfied with its position he closed the lid again and jogged the short distance back to the car.

He drove a couple of blocks down the road and reached the end of the neighborhood. He turned left and drove down one more block before deciding to pull over and stop again. Cranking his head over his shoulder he could just make out his target house off in the distance. At 10:30 he pushed the button on his remote and the mailbox to house 498 disappeared. He drove away quicker this time and headed for the nearest mall.

11

Stad stepped inside the large electronics store that anchored the mall and it felt like walking into a warehouse. The ceilings were high, the floor was concrete and the duct work was exposed.

"Need any help finding anything today?" A man in an orange shirt popped into view and got right to business. Stad brushed by him and pretended not to hear or see the man in the obnoxious shirt. He followed an aisle that led him to the television section full of small TVs, giant TVs and medium-sized TVs all of which were playing the latest and greatest movie on the latest and greatest movie player.

Stad continued down the path as it took a bend off to the left and passed movies, music and games. The path ended up taking him to the back of the store which housed the computer section. In the front area was a teenager who was behind a computer checking a spreadsheet and wearing the same annoying orange shirt. Stad was no more than three steps into the section when the teen employee turned around to greet him. His shirt was embroidered with "Troy" and Troy's smile seemed less than enthusiastic.

"Can I help you?"

"No, that's okay."

"If you need anything…" Troy's voice trailed off as Stad was already five computer cases into the closest row. At the end of that row he took a sharp right and found where they stored all the printers. There were inkjet printers, laser printers, photo printers, scanner printers, fax printers and every other imaginable kind except last year's model.

Stad hopped over to the next aisle where they kept all the ink and toner. He leaned in and examined the toners. He found a few different kinds that would work and he had come prepared for both, as was his usual mode of operation. He reached for one of the boxes and pulled it off its pronged display rack. Rotating it around in his hands he found the letters declaring it to be for only one kind of printer and that it could be recycled and how the company manufacturing it was going to save the world.

Stad sorted through all the mumbo jumbo and finally found what he had come here for. Below the recycling fluff and marketing nonsense, in tiny capital letters were the words "DO NOT EAT TONER." The warning was in black lettering surrounded by the white background of the box, so Stad removed the cap from his whiteout and edged the brush around and through the words, careful not to touch the surrounding letters. After going over it a few times Stad was convinced a customer wouldn't know the box had ever existed in any other state. He set the box face down on the floor, pulled the next one off the rack and continued to remove the warning for the four boxes left on the shelf. When finished, he placed each package back on the shelf one by one. He did a quick glance back at his handy work on his way out.

12

Indianapolis was no different than Dallas. There was a hotel, there were different women and there were days spent in a used car watching an empty house. His choice of target was different than the previous two and he had hoped to mix it up enough to keep any investigation on its toes. The neighborhood surrounding Durley Street wasn't wealthy but it wasn't poor either. The people who lived there made modest livings and for the most part lived from one paycheck to the next. The houses had imperfections and Stad felt more comfortable sitting around in the neighborhood for days.

On the day of the job he tried not to speed down the street as the events of the morning played out through his head.

"Are you going to call me?" she asked, standing next to the bathroom door.

"Probably not."

"Why not?"

"Probably because I don't live in town, I'm never here." Stad was starting to get frustrated.

"God, you men are all alike. All you want is sex and once you get that you don't give a shit about anything else."

"What do you want?"

"Someone who cares."

He had developed an art over the years of avoiding women like this, but for some reason it seemed like a good idea to him last night to bring her back to his room.

"That person's not here," he said.

"You're such an ass." She had been holding a towel but now it was flying toward Stad's face. He dodged it and managed not to spill any of his coffee.

"I've got things to do today, how much longer are you going to be yelling at me?" Another towel attacked his head.

"You should be ashamed of yourself. Grow up."

"Seriously though, are you going to leave soon?" Stad asked. She was out of towels so she stormed out.

Stad should have seen this one coming, but there wasn't anything he could do now and stepped on the gas to get over to the target on Durley. He approached the house and pulled over across the street. He was careful to stop in his legal parking spot before double checking to make sure there weren't any witnesses in the area. He leaned over and pulled out the package from beneath the passenger seat and began walking with it toward the target. He slid it into the mailbox and hurried back to his car. He drove off and only flinched when the shockwave caught up to him.

13

"Need a little help there?" Stad hopped up onto the leather upholstered barstool and swatted at the fly that had just landed on the counter in front of him. He was back home now after a long, monotonous flight and he could think of nothing better to do than to celebrate at his favorite bar.

Jones was crouched by the ice pit. "I think it's got a leak somewhere." The bartender stood up and Stad could see the wrinkles of his face thin out as he spread his old lips into a smile. "How you doing, Stad?" His hair was a messed up swirl, his beard was peppered and his eyes were tired.

"I've done better. Looks like you have too."

"Shouldn't be a huge problem, just got to fix it before it becomes one and we've got a lake on our floor."

"I don't think I could cope with that. I don't know where I'd go if you closed down the best jazz bar in town."

"Don't kid yourself, we all know you'd just spend more time across the street."

"Yeah that's true, I'd be over there in a heartbeat."

"How's work?" Jones asked, making Stad's drink.

"Same old I guess. Halfway through a big project and it's just kind of dragging me down, although I'm not sure how that's different than any other time."

"Yeah I know what you mean, it'd be nice to have a break every now and then, right? I had to let someone go last week and now I've got the pleasure of picking up that extra work myself. Just sucks sometimes, doesn't it?" He went back to mixing Stad's drink.

Stad wished he didn't have to be so vague. Over the years he had told Jones a lot about his fake accounting job and it was getting harder and harder to make sure he remembered everything. Every time he found himself in a corner he added more details like quirky coworkers, high-profile customers and fiery bosses and it was exhausting keeping them ready to be pulled out at any moment. Jones never pried too much though and didn't ask many follow-up questions outside of "Is that so?" or "Oh yeah?" As per usual, Stad tried to keep the conversation going by making sure the focus was always on the other person.

"Who'd you have to fire?"

"Some girl I hired just a few weeks ago. She couldn't control her attitude and got in fights with the customers, not a good thing for return business." Jones set the drink down on one of his name brand cardboard coasters.

"Ouch."

"We'll be all right, I've just been pretty busy trying to keep up with all the work and trying to find a replacement. I have to keep telling myself that it's only a job."

"At least you don't have to answer to anybody here, you're your own boss, you make the rules." Stad raised his glass to a toast nobody made and took a drink. "I'd kill for that."

"Trust me," Jones said, "it's not all it's cracked up to be. Lots of stuff that I have to put up with I never even thought about when I first started this place."

"I guess I could see that, but I'd love to be the one making the calls."

"I wish that's how it worked." Jones looked down at his leaky sink and shook his head before bending over to take a closer look. From behind the counter he projected his voice so Stad could hear. "Crowd should start coming in anytime now for happy hour, looks like you beat the rush today."

"Guess I have good timing." Stad faced the stage and listened to hi-hats and bass lines while he watched the crowd roll in.

14

After thousands of notes and a pair of drinks she walked into the bar. Her red top hugged her body in the same way her jeans did. She model walked her way up to the bar, her shoulder length brunette hair bounced to the rhythm of the Charlie Parker cover echoing off the walls. She leaned against the counter and flagged down Jones who was quick to rush to her call. Stad only pretended to pay attention to the solo on stage.

"Can I get a vodka martini?" She was one stool away from Stad but close enough for him to get a taste of her strawberry perfume.

"Yes ma'am."

"It's Nicole." She placed a 20-dollar bill on the counter.

"Jones," Stad said, "put it on my tab. He looked up at Nicole. "Don't worry about it."

"If you're trying to get in my pants, it's not going to happen."

"Hey." Stad surrendered. "I'm just offering to buy a nice lady a nice drink on a nice day."

"Well that's very *nice* of you, but I can take care of myself."

"All right, suit yourself, but I do have to warn you that Jones there," Stad pointed toward the bartender who had his back turned mixing the martini, "has been known to overcharge people he doesn't know."

"Is that so?" Nicole shot a glance toward Stad. "And how exactly would you know that?"

"I know him pretty well. You have to trust me on this one. It'll save you at least a dollar, maybe two."

"So you think I can't afford it?"

"I just think there are better ways to spend that money."

"Oh yeah? Any ideas?"

"Well I don't know you that well, but if I get to know you I'm sure I could offer up some suggestions."

"All right," she said, taking her 20 dollars off the counter. "That sounds fair. I'm Nicole, by the way."

"I know, I heard." He extended his hand. "Stad."

"Well thanks for the money-saving tip, Stad."

"Not a problem, I'd do it again if I had to."

"Here you go." Jones interrupted with a martini. As he walked away Stad could see the old man roll his eyes.

"So if I'm going to get to know you," Stad continued, "you should probably tell me why you're here. Are you a big jazz fan?"

"I'm impartial, but I'm supposed to be meeting up with some friends who really love it."

"They must have good taste."

"So I assume that's why you're here?"

"Partly, I've always loved jazz, but my job keeps bringing me back."

"Rough day?"

"You could say that." Stad swirled his scotch and seven.

"What makes them so rough?"

"For starters, I'm an accountant at an insurance firm."

"Ouch," Nicole said through a smile. "Those all sound like rough days to me."

"We can't all have exciting jobs like yours."

"I'm a real estate agent, and no, I won't give you any advice right now. It's after hours and you'll have to make an appointment."

"If that's how it's going to be, you can't ask me to do your taxes."

"Fair enough." Nicole took a drink before continuing. "So is that why you're able to get such good deals here? Are you cooking the books for this place or something?"

"Did the IRS send you?" They both laughed and Stad took a drink as the laughter began to fade. The entrance door opened and scattered light into the jazz-filled cavern. Both Stad and Nicole turned to see who the new guests were. Nicole flagged her friends down and Stad picked up his drink and watched the performance on stage. After some brief chatter about terrible traffic they all seemed to agree to find a seat.

"Okay," Nicole spoke up, "let me grab my drink and meet you over there." The three friends walked past Stad's line of vision and he watched them search for a table. Nicole turned back to the counter for her drink. "Hey Stad?"

His attention snapped back to Nicole.

"We're going to grab one of the booths," she said, pointing out the direction her friends were walking. "Thanks again for the drink."

"Anytime."

"I think I'll take you up on that. Plus you owe me some suggestions on how to spend my money, right?" Nicole reached for her purse and produced a pen. She grabbed the nearest coaster and scribbled on it before handing it to Stad.

"Call me." She smiled, collected her things and walked away, red top fading in the distance.

Most of happy hour was carried out by Stad enjoying the Miles Davis covers coming from the stage and talking to Jones when the bartender wasn't too busy getting drinks.

"So anyway," Jones projected over the 16 bar solo, "I said that if you can't pay your rent then I'm going to have to kick you out."

"Yeah."

"I didn't want to have to do it because she's a nice kid and didn't have any other places to go, but I just couldn't put up with it anymore."

"Yeah."

"Too much noise and racket and strangers coming and going."

"Yeah."

"Are you paying attention to me or staring at that girl in the red top?"

"Yeah, no, I would have done the same thing, Jones." Stad tilted his head back and finished off his latest drink. "Hey I'll be back. You better not give up this seat to the first hot woman that looks your way."

"I can't promise I won't."

"I wouldn't expect anything less from you." Stad jumped down from the barstool and weaved his way through the crowd to get to the bathroom. He crossed to the other side of the bar and couldn't help but glance over to the booth where Nicole and her friends were sitting.

The line was longer than he had ever seen it and by the time a urinal became available he thought he was going to explode. He rushed up to it and became the one that everybody was waiting on. He spent the time reading some of the postings on the corkboard above. There were ads for a band that needed a new bassist, a new bar opening up down the street, a great deal on piercings and a lecture taking place at the convention center. None of them were interesting to Stad so he finished and let another customer take his place.

On his way back he looked over to Nicole's table again. All he saw was an empty booth, so he took a closer look and didn't see any signs of their drinks or purses or previous presence.

"Hey," he said, trying to grab Jones' attention as he sat back down at his stool. "What do I have to do to get a drink around here?"

"All right, all right, calm down," Jones said, already reaching for the mixings.

"Make it a double."

"No problem." Jones poured in some extra scotch before sliding it over to Stad who picked it up and drank a third of it before setting it back down. The only thing Stad remembered the rest of the night was stumbling outside.

15

Stad woke up to a stranger next to him and he felt like his life was stuck on repeat. The only difference now was that he was in his own bed, which made him feel a little better. He walked out of his bedroom, made a brief detour to close the door to his office at the end of the hall and made his way to the bathroom. After splashing his face with cold water he trekked out to the kitchen where he prepped the coffee machine and waited for it to brew. Stad leaned against the granite-covered island while the machine chugged its way through the process and he stared out at the window at the far end of the living room. The window was large, almost floor to ceiling and wall to wall, and it allowed him to see the city in a way lots of people couldn't. Just beyond the glass were skyscrapers and rooftops and billboards and an endless supply of concrete. His life may be on repeat, but he never grew tired of this scene. He stared out at the details and searched for a new window or stain on a wall or a random piece of greenery breaking through the sidewalks.

The bold aroma of the coffee wafted his way and broke him away from his current fascination. He poured himself a generous cup and walked back to the window.

"How's the coffee?" A voice came from the hallway behind him.

"Hey," he said, turning around to see his guest in an oversized "Army" shirt. He looked down into the cup as if he was considering the question. "Not that good, actually. You probably don't want any."

"Oh."

"Hey, look." Stad walked back toward the island counter in the kitchen. "I've got this thing here in about half an hour or so, so do you have a ride home or anything?"

"Well, I don't have my car…"

"I'll leave you some money for a cab. I'd take you home myself but this thing is all the way across town and I really should be getting ready."

"Do you really have to go?"

"Afraid so."

"What are you doing tonight?"

"Hard to say, I've got another meeting this afternoon and it could run well into the night." Stad set his mug on the counter.

"Do you want to try and meet up for dinner or anything?"

"They're actually serving dinner there, so I don't think I'll be that hungry."

"What about lunch?" She pressed on.

"Client meeting, sorry."

"Well when are you free?"

"Yeah." Stad walked down the hallway and his voice grew louder. "I'm not really sure, what works for you?"

"I don't have a whole lot going on, do you want my number?" She tried to follow him but he was already back in the hallway.

"Yeah, that sounds great. Why don't you just leave it for me on the fridge or something? I don't have much for breakfast but help yourself to whatever you can find. I'm going to jump in the shower, you need anything?" He slapped two 20s on the counter. "If you do, just holler."

He headed into the bathroom and turned on the hot water. He could already hear her putting on her clothes. About the time he was rinsing the shampoo out of his hair he heard the door slam. He finished up and waited a few moments before coming out just to make sure she was really gone. Wrapped in a towel, he picked his mug back up and went over to his window to admire the view again.

16

Stad followed directions and took old route 14 to exit 23, then turned off on the dirt path that weaved back to the storage facility. There was no one near the entrance, just a beat up, rusted sign that greeted anybody who had property locked beyond the fence.

He found his way to unit #45 tucked away in the back row. He removed the giant lock and chain and rolled the door up into the ceiling, letting loose a strong smell of plastic and rubber. Inside, against the back wall, was a wooden table covered by an oversized black tarp. He walked over to it, flung the tarp to the side and revealed another package that he had become too familiar with in the past couple of weeks. He picked it up along with the little black box that was lying next to it on the table.

Bomb in hand, Stad headed back for his new used car and stopped at the passenger side door. He placed the package and detonator on the seat, being careful not to bump either against the hard plastic or the exterior of the car. The limits of the rusty chain were tested as Stad pulled it tight and far enough to lock the unit door back in place. After double checking the lock and checking it one more time, he got in his car and headed back toward old route 14. He veered off the 97th street exit and delved deeper into the suburbs where his car started to stick out more than he thought it would.

One picket fence led to another and the speed bumps were evenly spaced down the newly paved road. On one side there was a completed house with fresh sod, fresh paint and a fresh-faced family moving in. On the other side was a poured foundation surrounded by dirt. There were developments in all stages here and Stad passed them all until he got to Valley View Drive. The house number was 11242, a three-story white house with a bright red door that dared guests to enter. This house was isolated from all the others and surrounded by only a few foundations and some studs sticking out of the ground. Stad parked in the street in front of the half-completed house next to the target and stepped out with the package cradled in his arms. He walked up to the shiny mailbox that matched the color of the door and slipped the package inside.

Stad pulled away and drove down the smooth roads and past the houses yet to be built. When he was back on 97th street he pushed the button on the detonator. He took a quick glance in the rear-view mirror to see the smoke growing from where he had come from.

The building in front of Stad had no visible signs, markings, noticeable windows or individualistic flare and any tourist would only see it as a large cube in the middle of the city. He climbed the small set of steps out front and headed for the entrance. He pushed open one of the doors and walked across the smooth black marble floor that led to the lone security guard behind a square desk. The guard looked up from his post when he heard the sound of shoes tapping against the floor. His gray hair streaked out from underneath his standard issue hat and fell in front of the eyes sunk into his face. Stad approached and when he nodded in the guard's direction, the guard nodded back and returned to his paper.

Past the desk and to the right was a bank of six elevators. While he waited he checked his appearance in the shiny elevator doors. Sometime between checking his sweat-stained shirt and running his fingers through his hair a loud dinging sound came from above his head and one of the elevator doors slid open. Stad stepped inside, pressed the button for floor 18 and waited for the music-less elevator to take him to his destination.

When the doors opened again he was met with a blank wall of nothingness. There was no indication of where anyone was located on the floor, no directory, no receptionist, no floor plan, no plants, not even wallpaper, just a blank, gray wall. The only available option was to go left, which he did. The drab carpet of the hallway carried on for a while and when it came to an end he turned left. He turned left again when the second hallway ended and he found himself in front of a large, intimidating door. It looked like steel but he knew it wasn't. He leaned down near the tiny intercom speaker.

"Number 92." He didn't like the passphrase, but it was in use long before Stad got here, so he knew it wasn't going anywhere. The door clicked and Stad pushed it open and stepped into Max's office.

The first thing a guest saw was a wall of windows. They were above the entrance of the building but almost impossible to see from the outside because they were tinted black and matched the exterior so well. The windows carried to the end of the room at the far wall which contained nothing but monitors. The wall opposite the windows had filing cabinets lined up next to each other and in the middle of the room was Max's oversized stainless steel desk, which he was seated behind, holding a bottle of water.

"Water?" Max asked. A smile emerged from behind his rugged, unshaven face. His suit jacket and jean combination didn't quite match the rest of his mountain man appearance.

"No thanks." Stad slinked over to the desk and sat down opposite his boss.

"How'd it go?"

"Good. No problems, no incidents so far. What have you guys seen on your end?"

"Lots of stuff actually." Max shuffled through some of the papers sitting on the top of the desk before finding one that he brought closer to his face. "Mailbox explosion in Utah, another exploding house in central Florida, a headline stating 'Is there a serial bomber on the loose?' Lots of copycats already. That's only a list of a few but there are tons."

"What's the timing on those?"

"Nothing after Seattle but we did see a couple after Dallas and then a lot more after Indy. Things really picked up after the latest one on that development property."

"That's the easiest one to copy really, less risk, you know?"

"Yeah, so hopefully that'll boost our numbers even more. Looks like people are scared shitless now to even look at their mailbox let alone ship their holiday gifts that way. We haven't reached out to the delivery companies yet to get any indications on their numbers, but it's looking good."

"When are you guys doing that? It's kind of an important detail, just the whole reason we're doing this in the first place, right?"

"Probably within the next week or so. They wanted a boost for the holiday season and until that comes and goes they won't know for sure, but they'll have a pretty good idea."

"Are they withholding pay until then?"

"No." Max rested his elbows on the desk. "At least not all of it. We'll be getting half at the end of the week and the other half after the results are in after the holidays."

Perfect.

"Sounds good."

"Yeah, and while you're out spending all your money I've got something else for you to chew on." Max got up and walked over to one of the filing cabinets against the wall. He came back with a binder in his hand, sat down and slid it over to Stad. "We've got a big one coming our way this time. It's the beverage industry."

Stad flipped open the binder and started scanning some graphs and skimming through some paragraphs. He sifted through the information and hoped something would catch his eye.

"That document outlines the basic lay of the land in the industry as of today. To sum up, people want more water and less soda. Everyone is becoming more health conscious and turning to water and vitamin enhanced water and more or less dismissing soda altogether. The soda industry has taken a huge blow and has seen profits crash. They've approached us and want an idea of what it will take to get them back to previous profit levels."

"What are those?" Stad snapped into the conversation.

"It'd be an increase of four percent."

"That's pretty significant."

"That's part of the reason they came to us, they've heard we've done that in the past, which we have come close to. Remember the Tylenol scare of '82? Their market share dropped 22 percent and the competition got a five percent boost."

"That's pretty good, wish I would have been around for that one."

"Yeah, it was really good. It's a good case study but consumer reactions can go either way so it isn't rock hard science. Plus that was back before all the safety measures were really ramped up, so who knows anymore."

"We can take a look and see what we come up with." Stad closed the binder. "What's the timeline they're looking at?"

"They want to hit them right before water sales peak, so they're aiming for a summer strike, June or July. But of course that may be determined by what we end up doing as well, so we'll see. Either way you've got plenty of time and free rein on this one." Max's tension evaporated.

"I'll start when I get a chance and keep you updated when I find out more." Stad grabbed the binder and stood up. "Anything else?"

"That's all I got for you right now. There's a bunch of good information in there, so it's a good place to start."

"All right." Stad started heading for the door. "Max." He stopped and turned to face his boss standing behind the desk. "Don't forget to call me when the first payment comes in."

"Why, did you burn through all your money again?" Max laughed. Stad just smiled and turned back around to walk out the door. "Take care out there, Stad."

"You too, boss." The door closed behind him and sent a thunderous echo down the hallway.

18

The temperature outside continued to fall alongside Stad's bank account balance. Max had made sure it was infused with cash for the hard work on the delivery company job, but Stad always managed to burn through it. Because of the nature of his job he had to keep a low profile and couldn't upgrade his apartment or buy a new high-end car or spend larger than normal chunks of it at a time. These limitations required him to spend it how he knew best, so he was in and out of Jones' on a regular basis. The changing weather and accumulating snow tended to keep people away and in their cozy homes, including the women that Stad had a tendency to hook up with. A few times he had seen women who ventured out to the bars and about half of the time they would have to find their way back from Stad's place. His average was down during the winter, but that was to be expected.

One of the mornings that he found himself alone in his bed, he dragged himself out and across the cold floor to the kitchen for some breakfast. He searched in the cabinets and the fridge and realized that he had nothing to eat and needed to make a quick run to the store, so he threw on some clothes and a jacket and stepped out into the frigid air.

On the way there he couldn't help but feel guilty that he hadn't done any work on the new job that Max had given him.

With the success and relative ease of all of his recent jobs he had become lazy and today was the first time he started to worry that he was falling behind. After all, it had been quite a while since he received the information, maybe he should take a look at it again. He knew he needed to pick up the pace and vowed to start as soon as he got back.

The parking lot was plowed pretty well and there weren't too many cars so he grabbed a spot close to the door and made his way to the entrance. He picked up a basket and headed for the back corner of the store to pick up some cheese, a dozen eggs and a gallon of milk. He turned around and walked the back linoleum-lined row of the store with aisle after aisle of consumable crap. He ducked into a couple of aisles here and there to pick up cereal, pasta and a few frozen dinners and then wandered over to where they kept the snack food. It was the last thing he had to pick up and was in such a hurry to get out of the store that he almost bowled over an elderly woman reaching for a bag of walnuts on the top shelf. She took a step back in surprise.

"Can you reach those walnuts for me?" Her voice was no more audible than a whisper.

"Oh, sorry, wrong aisle." Stad avoided eye contact and looked up at the sign above the aisle as the words came out of his mouth. Halfway through his sentence he had already started to turn around and walk the other way. He didn't look back to see the disappointment in the old woman's face. He headed down the next row over and hoped the old lady would get ahold of her walnuts so he would be free to roam for junk food again. He was now facing a row of bread and since he was here he decided to toss a loaf in his cart, because who couldn't use bread? He went to reach for one when he heard a voice from behind him.

"Stad?"

He turned in the direction his name came from. Outside of one night stands nobody around town knew him. He hoped it wasn't one of the crazy women he had disappointed, seeking revenge for not being the perfect man they wanted him to be. Standing there holding a red basket with only a few items, was a gorgeous, somewhat familiar woman with short brunette hair.

"Hey." His brain scrambled to make the connection.

"You never called." She began walking toward him.

"Nicole…" Her familiar strawberry perfume landed on his nose and his brain managed to make the connection back to Jones' and the vodka martini he had paid for.

"Nikki. You can call me Nikki."

"Yeah, sorry about that." He struggled to find the right words. "Things at work just kind of got busy so I got caught up in it and never called. You know how it is."

"So busy that you're out on a Tuesday morning doing your grocery shopping?"

"I took the day off." His brain raced again to find an ending to the sentence. Would she care why he was out and about? Would it make sense to say he was sick? If that was the case, why would he be shopping for bread? "I have to run home after this, my heat stopped working and I'm just killing time before the repair guy can make it out there."

"That sucks, hope it gets fixed, it's pretty cold out."

"Wait a minute, what are *you* doing here on a Tuesday morning?"

"I work in real estate, remember? I usually make my own office hours, and since nobody wants to look for houses when there's a foot of snow on the ground, it's been pretty slow lately."

"Must be nice."

"Sometimes." Nikki shrugged. "What are you doing tomorrow night? Any plans?"

"Nothing that I know of." He always tried to avoid dates, but sometimes he wasn't quick enough to come up with an excuse and they just snuck up on him.

"Do you want to grab something to eat?"

Backed into a corner.

"Sure."

"I mean, you still have to get to know me, right? That one dollar you saved me is burning a hole in my pocket." Nikki moved her head to get her hair out of her eyes.

"Yeah, I bet."

"I know a great place downtown on 20th if you like Italian."

"Oh yeah, Magiattos? They have really good bread."

"People keep recommending it to me, and you make one more, so it must be a sign. What time works best for you?"

"Anything really. What about seven?" Stad asked.

"I can make that work. I may have to meet you there, is that all right?"

"Yeah." That was preferred. "But right now I better get back to my place, don't want to keep the maintenance man waiting."

"Good luck with that."

"Thanks." Stad smiled and started to walk away.

"See you tomorrow," Nikki called out. Stad just nodded and went straight for the self-checkout lane.

***

Stad diverted from his usual route back home and wound up at a grocery store that looked like it hadn't been updated since the 70s. He spent five minutes weaving in and out of messy rows until he came to one that seemed to be dedicated to nothing but fruit snacks. He inspected one from random off the shelf and after a few moments, found text on the back that seemed so small he thought it should be illegal. He squinted as he read "REMOVE PLASTIC BEFORE EATING."

He traced over the words to form a perfect, dark rectangle where the words had once been and continued down the row until he reached the back of the shelf. He finished up and aligned them all again so that even the most anal retentive stocker wouldn't notice anything.

He walked away from the scene hoping he helped to improve the world's IQ by at least a couple of points. On his way out he grabbed a bag of potato chips that he missed at the first store.

19

A bunch of suits were seated around a giant oak table. Each suit was a different shade of dark blue, some fading into black and others fading into a darker black. The man at the head of the table had the blackest suit of them all. He had a fresh cigarette between his fingertips and he was slouched in his chair. He leaned forward to tap his ashes in the ashtray in front of him. The squeak against the leather seemed to drag on for days.

"Tell me something good." His voice was low and belonged to a lifelong smoker. His words were directed at the only female in the room who was seated to his left. Everyone in the room knew she had slept with someone to get the job and were all hoping she was open to promotions. She flung strands of hair from her eyes and cleared her throat.

"Recent numbers show that sales came in lower than the expected holiday numbers for us while the movie industry came in above projections." Her eyes moved from the papers resting on the polished table in front of her to Suit #1, the smoker at the head of the table. His expression hadn't changed in the past 40 years so she kept talking.

"According to our latest numbers, the average American family just isn't willing and can't justify the purchase of the latest technology in home theater entertainment. They are, however, willing to spend that money going out to the movies." She glanced across the table to the men who happened to be there, one of whom was bald, the other balding and the third man with a bad toupee. Their suits were royal blue, navy blue and royal navy blue. Their expressions were as cold and empty as the closets their suits hung in.

"It would appear at first glance that movie ticket sales are decreasing, however, studios are producing blockbusters and franchises that continually draw in large crowds. Because of this, they are breaking all records across the board but we are unable to firmly draw a conclusion that these records are or are not merely a misinterpretation of numbers. Since admission prices are rising in step with record numbers it is tough to separate the two." She paused for a moment to take a sip of water from her glass and to let her words soak into the minds of the suits. They tended to be slow in understanding some things, but even if there was a misunderstanding they wouldn't bring it up in front of their other suit friends.

"In addition to the blockbusters, franchise powerhouses and new technology, we are also looking into the latest luxury theaters that have been popping up in the country. Five nationwide chains have appeared over the last six months and ten more are expected over the next year. Their popularity is increasing and gaining momentum even though these theaters charge on average, five dollars more per showing."

"Are those the ones with fancy meals and furniture and what not?" Suit #1 leaned forward and placed his forearms on the table.

"Correct. They have full course meals which are also more costly than an average restaurant and they provide tables and chairs to enjoy the night out. Specific times are usually reserved for couples as well as family times and kids' specials."

"Bullshit." The room could tell Suit #1 was angry by the way the words leaked out of his mouth and into the smoke-filled air hovering around him. The men at the table were unflinching in response to the boss' profanity and instead nodded in agreement with it. Suit #1 took a long drag, exhaled again and stared at nothing in particular. "What about our profits?"

"Despite not meeting expectations last quarter, over the year profits increased around two percent."

Suit #1 balanced his cigarette on the ashtray and then clasped his hands together and flattened them against the table. He cracked his knuckles, picked up his cigarette and inhaled again. He was a man of few words, but when he spoke people listened and always interpreted the smallest hint of negativity as a terrible, horrible catastrophe. His extended silence caused non-audible murmurs from the other suits.

"Not good enough." Suit #1's eyes shifted from the woman on his left to the three men on his right, known only to him as the Three Bald Mice. "What have you got for me?"

The Mice shuffled through a couple of folders and laid out some papers on the table. The baldest of them spoke first.

"We would first like to show you the idea that we think has the most potential."

20

"Sorry I'm running behind," Stad said between gasps of air as he walked up to the table.

"That's okay, I haven't been waiting long." Nikki was wearing a snug sweater and a nice pair of gray pants that Stad could see on her crossed legs underneath the table. He took his coat off and put it on the back of his chair and inhaled her scent of strawberry perfume. He didn't remember smelling it anywhere else which probably meant it was too expensive or too cheap.

"Have you ordered anything yet?"

"Just this water." She brought the glass to her seductive red lips and took a drink. Right on cue, as if waiting off stage and listening to every word, the server approached the table in a white shirt and black apron.

"Can I get you anything to drink, sir?"

"I'll have water also and a bottle of wine, from somewhere in France."

"May I suggest a Burgundy pinot?"

"That sounds great, thank you."

The waitress walked away.

"What sounds good?" Stad picked up the menu, only now getting to see what was on the list.

"It all *sounds* good, and I'm assuming from the look of this place that it all *is* good."

Nikki was right. Magiattos seemed impressive. Stad glanced around and noticed the white silk linens, the dim candlelight, the marble floors, the artwork hanging on the oak walls and the classical music playing through hidden speakers. He had been here before but still hadn't figured out if it was actually fancy or just trying to be fancy.

"Yeah, I don't think you can go wrong here," he said.

"I'm thinking about the chicken parm for now, what about you?"

"I'm a sucker for lasagna so I think I'm just going to stick with the classic, but honestly I could just have the bread for a meal."

"Yeah, it is really good, you need to eat all of it before I do. Besides, the prices aren't on here, so maybe all we can afford is the bread."

"You've got that extra dollar in your wallet though, right?" Stad smiled and Nikki returned a polite laugh. "So what'd you think of Jones'?"

"I liked it. My coworkers had recommended the place so I couldn't turn it down. Most of us had actually never been there so it was an experience. I didn't think I'd like it since I don't usually like places like that…" She paused and tried to backpedal. "Not that I'm saying it's a bad place, but I just prefer-"

"I know what you mean. And you don't have to worry about offending me. I think I've only ever been offended once and it was back in the 80s."

"Sorry, I-"

"Really Nikki, you don't have to be. As long as you had a good time there."

"I did. The music was amazing, the drinks were great, tell Jones I said that."

"He'll be happy to hear."

"Plus it's easy to get to for all of us."

"Don't you all work with each other though?" Stad asked.

The waitress interrupted the conversation carrying Stad's water and a bottle of wine. She memorized the orders then fled the scene.

"Sorry, forgot what we were talking about," Nikki said.

"I was just wondering why you and your coworkers didn't just travel together, seeing as how you all work together. I thought that'd be easier for everyone."

"Oh yeah, well we share a common office but we're not all there at the same time most of the time. Another downfall of the business I'm in, I don't get to see my coworkers as often as I would like."

"Other than that how are things?" Stad picked up another slice of bread and set it on the tiny plate in front of him.

"It's been interesting. It's definitely a bigger market than what I'm used to. I just moved into town maybe … three months ago?"

"In that case welcome to the city. Where'd you move from?"

"I wasn't much further away actually, maybe an hour south into the suburbs. So I can't say I'm new here, I just requested a move to get more opportunities, but thanks anyway. It's been a pretty rough start so far. I haven't sold much since it's not a great season to sell houses and I had the weirdest thing happen to another one of my properties. You know those mailbox bombs that have been all over the news? One of them was at a place I was trying to sell. It was a new construction project out on Valley View of all places."

"Wow." Stad took another bite from his bread.

"Yeah, apparently there's some sort of movement going around where people are blowing up mailboxes. I don't know but I was pretty pissed about it."

"Yeah that's not good, sorry to hear that."

"Yeah, I'll recover it's just a pain in the ass, you know? I don't even know why anyone would want to do it. Nobody was living there. It was probably just a bunch of bored teenagers."

"Yeah…" Stad's voice faded into his water glass.

"They seemed to have stopped though so hopefully I won't have to go through that again."

"You'll probably be fine. So I've always wondered, how does it work, selling houses? Do you and your coworkers split areas or something, or do you get the short stick since you're the new person?"

"We kind of split things here and there." She fiddled with the napkin in front of her. "It really depends on what we need at the time, so it's hard to say. What about you? How's work?"

"Pretty slow, as you could probably tell from my grocery outing yesterday."

"Oh yeah, did you get your heater fixed?"

"Yeah, I'm warm again, thanks."

"Sorry to cut you off, I was just curious. So you're an accountant you said, right? What's that like?"

"You know, it's just work. It's pretty boring stuff other than the occasional travel, but that's pretty rare."

"Travel? I didn't think accountants got to go anywhere. I thought they kept you guys locked up in the basement with calculators and spreadsheets." Nikki laughed.

"You'd be surprised. Sometimes I have to go to a client's site to review their numbers and stuff like that. They've really tightened the reins on us since a whole bunch of companies were caught cooking the books." Stad ad-libbed between buzzwords. "Is there any particular reason you go by Nikki or is it mostly for convenience?"

"I don't really like my full name." She sipped her wine. "It has too much of a professional ring to it. Not that that's bad, but cutting it short makes it sound more fun, you know?"

"Yes, I do. I don't really like my name either but it can't be cut much shorter."

"Stad? You don't like that?"

"You do? I guess it's already short and kind of like a nickname, I've just never met anyone else with it. I'm convinced my parents were either drunk or lost in Europe when they picked it out." Stad laughed and Nikki followed right along.

"Have you asked them?" She leaned forward in the booth, sending a breeze of strawberry air swirling in Stad's direction.

"Well, I never actually knew them." He took a large sip of wine. "They died when I was young."

"Oh Stad, I'm sorry."

"It's okay. It was a long time ago and you know, how can you miss someone you never really knew?"

"I'm really sorry. If I would have known I never would have brought that up."

"How could you have known? Don't worry about it."

***

The food arrived not much longer and they dined over conversation. Stad didn't have too much to say, especially about personal topics, but he found that it came easy around Nikki. Of course he didn't share too many details and kept everything focused on her, but he was having fun and was able to let his guard down just a little bit. He couldn't remember the last time he had been in this position with anyone. They touched on everything including family, previous relationships, movies, books and which famous dead people they'd like to invite to dinner. The waitress came and went with the bill and they kept talking.

After a while nothing was left on their plates but scraps and streaks of pasta sauce. The wine had been consumed long ago and the ice in their water glasses was beginning to melt and pool in the bottom. It was close to ten thirty and they were lost in conversation when the server came up to the table.

"Excuse me," she said. "We'll be closing in five minutes."

"I suppose that means we should get out of here?" Stad turned to Nikki.

"I was thinking, if you're up for it, we could have some coffee at my place?" Nikki asked, but the way the words came out, Stad knew it wasn't a question.

"I would need a ride if you're offering."

"Sure, I'm parked right out front." She picked up her purse and coat. "Let's get out of here."

The ride to her place wasn't too far but it was an area that Stad had never ventured. It was north off the interstate, past the noise and lights and graffiti-covered billboards pitching everything from new coffee flavors to sparkling jewelry to the gang off 13th street. Her sedan twisted and turned and handled the bumps and ice patches in the city streets with ease. Stad had lost track of where he was but he always knew which direction they were traveling.

"How far out of town is it?" he asked.

"It's not much further. I really wanted a place closer to downtown, but since I moved on such short notice there wasn't much available." She pulled the car off onto a driveway and passed a sign that said "Parkview Place." A six-story apartment building came into view. Half of the rooms had balconies that overlooked a park and decent-sized pond and the others had a view of an empty field.

"I thought you had a house."

"I'm in the process of buying one. I have everything set up, but again, because of the short notice I'm renting until everything's finalized."

"How do you like it here?" Stad asked.

"It's not too bad, but I'm not a huge fan of apartment living." Nikki parked the car and they got out.

"A little colder than I thought it would be." Stad regretted not bringing a warmer coat as they hustled to the elevators. They didn't have to wait too long before the elevator doors opened and they stepped inside and out of the cold. As the doors were sliding shut Nikki turned to Stad and lunged forward at him. Her lips ran into his and they kissed until they were on the sixth floor.

"So I guess this means no coffee?" Stad asked. Nikki grabbed his hand and dragged him to her door.

21

Stad woke up in a sea of billowing sheets and strawberry air. The white ceiling fan swirled above and provided just enough of a breeze to remind him that he wasn't wearing a shirt. Next to him was a motionless mess of brunette hair protruding from the crumpled sheets. His eyes traced upward, past the tuft of hair to the alarm clock resting on the night stand. After seeing it was 7:30 his eyes kept wandering and found a door on the other side of the room that he remembered led to the bathroom. He eased out of the sheets and sat at the edge of the bed trying to get his bearings.

The floor was covered in nothing, a sight unseen at Stad's place, and the walls matched the bareness with no family pictures, abstract art or paint that wasn't white. Other than the bed, the only other item in the room was a dresser next to an open closet that contained a few pieces of clothing that appeared to be organized by color.

Stad stood up, stretched his legs and saw the only mess in the room. In the corner, on the floor was a tangled pile of clothes. He rummaged through them, digging past Nikki's outfit from last night, until he found his shirt and jeans. He tossed his clothes aside and headed for the bathroom.

He turned the knob and hoped the hinges didn't groan like his. The door complied and swung open in silence and revealed the most immaculate bathroom Stad had ever seen. It seemed as though it had never been used and was straight out of a cleaning product commercial. He wouldn't be surprised if he saw a sparkle glimmer off the countertop. The toilet was so clean and shiny that he felt guilty taking a piss in it. He flushed and grabbed a tissue, blew his nose and went to throw it away in the trashcan by the shower but hesitated. He wanted to pull back the polka-dotted shower curtain and see what the tub was like. Everything was so perfect, but something had to be off, right? Nobody was this clean. After a few moments he decided it was going to be nothing but perfect, so he threw the tissue away and walked over to the sink. He stood in his boxers, scratched his stubble and wondered what he had gotten into. He wasn't supposed to go on dates, let alone sleep over at his date's apartment. He snapped out of his trance, splashed his face and cleared his throat. He opened the door and saw Nikki sitting up in the bed.

"Good morning." Her eyes were still adjusting to the light.

"Right back at you." Stad realized he was in nothing but his boxers, so he took three giant strides across the room to get to his clothes.

"Oh shit," Nikki muttered. "I've got to get to work." In one motion she pulled the sheets away from her body, jumped up and leapt into the bathroom in her skimpy pair of underwear. Across the room Stad slipped his legs into his pants, tossed his shirt over his head and put on his shoes, foregoing the socks which had gone missing some time last night.

"Hey Nikki," he hollered. The bathroom door inched open and Nikki's head peaked out. "I'm going to take off."

"Ok, do you need a ride?"

"No, I'll catch a cab."

"You sure? It's not that big of a deal for me."

"Don't worry about it." Stad made his way to the bedroom door. "I don't want to get in your way or anything. Not a big deal."

"All right." She closed the door.

Success. They were on the same page.

Stad left the room, happy that Nikki didn't want anything to do with him this morning either. The hallway led to a living room which contained an empty bookshelf, a TV, a few scattered magazines on the table in front of a plush couch and a floor lamp tucked away in the furthest corner. The kitchen rivaled the bathroom in cleanliness and if Stad didn't know any better he would have guessed nobody lived here at all. Or maybe somebody just slept here and didn't do much else.

He opened the door and stepped out into a miserable morning. It was cold, drizzling snow and much earlier than he was used to. He shut the door and headed for the elevator where his crazy night started in the first place. He pulled out his cell phone and dialed the local cab company. The elevator took him to the ground level and he waited for the taxi and rested on a chilled bench by the pond that was on the verge of freezing over. He was cold again and still wishing for a heavier coat.

The cab finally pulled up and Stad picked himself up off the bench and hopped into the uncomfortable, but warm backseat.

"Take me to the closest department store."

22

"Keep the meter running." Stad reached for his wallet and pulled out two 20-dollar bills. He handed them over to the cab driver, stepped out into the cold and headed for the entrance of the store in front of him. The automatic doors slid open and Stad walked past the clerk at the one open register.

He breezed by the sorry excuse for a cafeteria with week-old hot dogs and past the accessories department with unwanted jewelry and tacky handbags. He walked past the electronics full of unplayable games and outdated CDs and past the tiny book section displaying the latest bestsellers, celebrity books and nothing in between. He kept going past the housewares department with cheap silverware and moved down the aisle past the men's clothing section with only small and extra-large sizes.

He navigated the maze of the store and when he passed the kids' toys tainted with lead section he arrived at the small appliance area in the far corner. He followed the floor to where the irons were kept and grabbed one off the shelf. He read the back of the box to make sure it was what he wanted and confirmed it with the warning label on back that read "Warning: Never iron clothes on the body." Stad grabbed his handy black marker, pulled off the cap and colored in the warning label. He set that box on the floor, grabbed the next box on the shelf and covered that warning label too. He did the same for the third one before putting all the boxes back in their rightful spots.

23

Stad decided to stop procrastinating and work on the new job. He already had a good grasp on the soda industry because of his case study on the New Coke release back in the 80s but he knew much less about bottled water. In recent years however, he knew that the two industries had started merging and some were now operating under mega corporations. Stad made a note to clarify that it would be hard to separate the two for the job and that it was possible that both divisions could be harmed no matter how many precautions he took.

The growth percentage that the soda industry requested was within reach, but the aggressiveness of it increased the risk factor by a large margin. The only redeeming factor to the risk would be pay, which Stad expected would be quite high for a case like this. The biggest payout he had been involved in had been in the millions split between Stad's supplier, the parent company, Max, Stad and some of the other agents. He always wondered what kind of justification the companies had for return on investment on jobs like that.

Unsure of what to target first, Stad pulled some SEC filings, marketing profiles, demographics, sales charts, reports and advertising trends. With such a broad range he was hoping to hit something, but the only thing he was able to confirm was that the industry was growing around one percent per year and they were targeting health-conscious consumers. The information wasn't much help and as the sun went down behind the skyline Stad began to get coffee jitters, so he got up and brewed a pot.

Stad sat back down in his executive leather chair, sipped his coffee and pulled up his contact list. He dialed the top number.

"Yeah?" A raspy voice answered after the ninth ring. In the background some rummaging could be heard along with the sound of a door closing.

"It's Stad."

"It's been a while. You get everything?"

"Without any hitches."

"Good to hear. You got the payment for it yet?"

"No, we haven't received it all."

"When are you supposed to?" The man on the other line coughed.

"Should be in within a couple of weeks. Don't worry about it, you'll get yours."

"I always have. So what do you need this time?"

"I'm just looking for some information right now. Memos and lawsuit documentation if you can get it." There was a long silence as Stad drank his coffee.

"Yeah, yeah, no problem. What's the story?"

Stad gave a shortened version of Max's spiel as well as the timeline he was working with. He left a few spots blank and let his supplier fill them in with his own ideas.

"All right, seems like something we should be able to pull off. I'll send you that documentation tonight. Shouldn't be more than an hour. Same encryption and password as last time."

"Thanks." Stad trusted his supplier as a man of his word, no matter how many words it was. He waited for the documentation and double checked the initial sales analysis and ran profile sweeps on all employees within the top players of the industry, specifically targeting upper management. Most everyone came back clean other than the ordinary speeding or parking ticket and a couple of outlier charges for domestic abuse, DUIs and a battery case. Almost on the hour from his phone call an encrypted email arrived in his inbox with the simple subject line of "Data." Stad downloaded it, entered the password and started to pore over the documents.

About two hours and another coffee pot into the process he noticed a trend of fear. Environmental groups had started to voice their opinions and the industry was afraid their sales would suffer. One memo cited studies that showed the waste from bottled water caused tremendous negative impact to the environment. According to another memo and cross-referenced with an archived newspaper article, one company was under a boycott from an environmental protection group a few years ago. That boycott didn't amount to much and eventually fizzled out but stirred up even more fear throughout the industry.

Stad leaned back in his chair and rubbed his eyes to give them a rest. The environment angle was a good one, but not good enough to get people to stop using the product. To get people to voluntarily quit something had proven difficult in the past, which was why most jobs now almost always included some sort of physical threat. Even though it was weak, he jotted down the idea on his list of potentials and then got up and walked around his apartment for a while.

It was well into the night when Stad came across a gold mine. It was a memo, dated 1996, that showed evidence that the then CEO for the largest bottled water company tried to cover up the fact that their water was nothing more than tap water from local sources. The memo went on to say that the company tried to suppress a third party investigation into the matter. Stad was quick to run some searches for the third party investigators and anything related to the year 1996 but came up with no significant findings. The company must have done an awful good job of covering it up. It wasn't that Stad needed the information, it just sparked an idea that he couldn't get away from. Tap water was seen as more contaminated than bottled water, but what if the so-called purified water itself was contaminated? His mind raced to the Tylenol scare Max had talked about. He knew there were logistical nightmares, but it seemed like a simple solution. He would just need to contaminate some batches, spread the news and let consumer panic take over. It wasn't guaranteed that the impacted clients would move to soda, but it could be argued that there wasn't any way that could ever be guaranteed.

Stad bumped this idea to the top of the list and scribbled a few notes in the whitespace next to it. It seemed like a good place to take a break for the evening.

24

"Busier than usual?" Stad leaned in to get Jones' attention.

"It's a Saturday night, tough to predict. You missed a great gig last night."

"Wish I could have been here."

"Work keeping you around late?"

"That and the bitter cold keep me inside, but you know how it is, every now and then I need a stiff drink."

"Well I hope this one does the trick." Jones slid Stad's usual to him. "How's the love life? You know I have to live through you."

"I was on a date not too long ago."

"A date? That's not usually how you roll. I would expect it to be something like you met her, took her back to your place, had a long and sleepless night, she leaves in the morning and you haven't seen her since."

"We actually ended up at her place, but that's not the point."

"That's always the point with you." Jones laughed. "Just come back when you've had another date and we'll talk."

"I mean, yeah, usually that's what happens, but I ran into her and she suggested a date. What am I supposed to do, say no?"

"Yeah, I guess that's not really an option." Jones broke eye contact and looked around for other customers. "Who was it with anyway? I know her?"

"I met her here, you might remember her. Nicole, smells like strawberries."

"Oh yeah, she's damn hot."

"Yeah, and she said she likes your drinks."

"What'd I make her?" Jones asked.

"Vodka martini, I think."

"Oh yeah, those are pretty popular around here. I get lots of practice. So you take her out to a nice place?"

"Magiattos, on her recommendation." Stad sipped from his scotch and seven.

"She must have been looking for a romp too. Stad the player, I wouldn't expect anything else."

"Yeah," Stad muttered.

"That's enough for me to live through for one night." Jones pointed to the drink in Stad's hand that was almost gone. "That one's on the house."

"Thanks."

Stad was several drinks deep when the clock rolled around past midnight. He struck up conversations with a few of the women that ventured toward his end of the bar whether on purpose or not. Some of them had interesting stories but Stad found most of them dull and tuned them out within the first five minutes.

What a shitty night.

He threw down the final half of his last glass and wobbled out into the snowy street.

25

The Three Bald Mice were standing, facing Suit #1. The one in the middle was holding a piece of paper with numbers and graphs as the baldest one on his left explained them. The right most one stood there and pointed to whatever the baldest one was talking about.

"So as you can see, if we lower our prices a mere five percent we can attract a much larger user base and draw in new customers." Mouse #1 tried to crack a smile and watched for Suit #1's reaction. The paper being held by Mouse #2 was shaking and Mouse #3 was wringing his hands. The man at the head of the table held his chin in his hand and rested it against his protruding gut. He scanned the chart and from time to time would let out a soft, thoughtful grunt. Between his grunting was a sound so silent that the ashes from his cigarette could be heard falling into his ashtray. After decades of everyone staring at him staring at a piece of paper, his eyes started to wander around the table. He stopped at the woman next to him for a while and looked for any clues she might hold to this puzzle before going around the table. He finally settled on the graph rattling around in Mouse #2's hands.

He reached out toward his ashtray and grasped his dwindling cigarette in his stubby pointer and middle fingers. He drew it to his mouth and took a long puff. The embers reflected in the polish of the oak table beneath. With a powerful exhale he added a new layer of smoke to the dingy room. The smoke wafted toward the assistant and she was careful not to flinch and draw unwanted attention to herself.

"No," he said, leaning against the table, still holding the cigarette between his fingers. He tapped the ashes from his cigarette and took another draw. There were no choruses of "But we worked months on this. You can't just turn it down like that. What if we just lower it three percent?" The Three Bald Mice stood firm and accepted defeat. With all eyes on them again, they perspired more than usual and their collective heads reflected the lights from above and caused a strong glare from any angle.

"We have also looked into expanding marketing efforts as well as partnering with a broader range of industries." While Mouse #1 was giving his speech, #2 and #3 were rummaging through the papers scattered in front of them. Mouse #2 produced the proper poster for this section of the presentation and Mouse #1 kept talking. "According to our research, homes with a pool table are twice as likely to have already purchased a home entertainment system or willing to purchase one. Another study we conducted shows that homes with pets-"

"This is the stupid." Suit #1 cut off the speaking mouse. #2 was shaken and dropped the paper to the table. #3 stood there not knowing what to do next. #1 finally recovered and spoke up again.

"We have also-"

"No, I don't want to hear from you anymore." Suit #1 tapped his forefinger on the table in a rhythmic pattern, mimicking a leaky faucet. He took the last drag from his cigarette and smashed it against the bottom of the tray. He produced another one from the pack lying on the table and his assistant offered a lighter. "Anyone else?" His voice sounded rougher than before from the latest conquered cigarette. A man at the opposite end of the table moved in his chair and in an instant, all eyes were fixed on him.

"I think I might know a way sir." His voice pinned him as middle aged, weary from long hours at the office and desperate for attention from the boss. He was a black suit wearer with slick backed dark hair and facial features that used to be chiseled.

"Yeah?" Suit #1 addressed the newcomer.

"What if we just sabotage the movie industry?" The room fell silent again. After two meticulous puffs on his cigarette and dispensing of ashes, Suit #1 voiced his opinion.

"I like it."

26

Stad woke up to the sound of his phone ringing on the night stand. He stumbled out of bed and reached for it to stop the blaring noise.

Who's calling this early?

"Hello?" He glanced at his clock and realized it was after noon.

"Hey Stad, it's Nikki."

"Oh hey, it's been a while, what's up?" In his haze he struggled to remember if he had given her his phone number.

"Interested in catching a movie tonight?"

"Um, sure. What do you have in mind?" Stad rubbed his face and tried to focus on the conversation. She was the last person he expected a call from.

"What do you think about 'Flight 817'?" she asked.

"Yeah, that's fine."

"Great."

"I can pick you up if you want."

"Actually," she said, "what do you think about grabbing some food first then heading out from there?"

"That works."

"Okay great, because I've been told there's a great pizza place downtown that I have to try. Ever heard of 'PJs Pizza'?"

"Oh yeah, it's not too far from my apartment either. I never realized I lived so close to all these recommended restaurants."

"Yeah, I guess so. Want to meet there around, let's say 5:00?"

"5:00 works for me. I guess I'll see you then."

"All right Stad, can't wait. Talk to you then."

"Bye." Stad slammed his phone back on his nightstand and his head back into the pillow. He was surprised to hear from her. The two had a good time at dinner a while ago, but he didn't think much of it afterwards. He thought they had parted ways with the same expectations but apparently she wanted something more. After a few minutes of rest he popped up out of bed and flung his curtains open. The day was gray and the melting snow caused rivers to run through the roads. Neon signs declared businesses to be open or closed and cars clogged the slushy streets. He hopped in the shower before falling into the kitchen for a pot of coffee to get his day started.

He got lost among his research papers as he delved further into the water industry job and before he could make a sizeable dent into some more memos, 5:00 showed up on his clock and he had to rush to get to PJs on time.

"You have a bad habit of showing up late, don't you?" Nikki asked as Stad approached her booth from the door.

"Not always, I'll work on it, promise." He sat down on the hard green plastic just as the waiter showed up in his company standard forest green shirt to take drink orders. They both ordered water.

"How's your weekend been so far? I mean, outside of tonight of course."

"Of course," she responded. "It's going pretty well. I had to work for a while yesterday and that was pretty miserable actually. Everything's just kind of slushy and wet, makes for terrible showings."

"Yeah, I bet."

"And I had to get some paperwork done at the office so I was pretty busy all day." She let out a big sigh.

"That's a lot of weekend work for no overtime pay."

"Yeah, but I'm trying to make a good impression underneath this new manager so hopefully I'll be on the radar for a promotion."

"That seems pretty aggressive for a new team member. I mean, not that I don't think you deserve it, it's just a little quick, don't you think?"

"Well I'm new to this office but I've been with the same company for four years now. I think I'm due for a promotion. I've gotten smaller ones here and there but nothing major. Kind of like spackling over some holes in a wall rather than building a new one."

"A house analogy. Those must go over really well in your line of work," Stad joked.

"For you information, they do. But seriously, don't you think I deserve a promotion after four years?"

"If I were your boss you would have already gotten one."

"Well thanks, even though I know that would be coming from a biased boss."

The waiter reappeared with the waters. "Have you decided what you would like?" The server leaned over and placed the dripping glasses on the laminate-covered table.

"Yeah, I've had some time to look it over and I think the Vivacious Veggie sounds good. Sound okay to you?" Nikki looked over at Stad.

"Sure." He couldn't tell if she was just stating a fact that she had had time to look over the menu or if it was a jab at him for being late. Regardless, he didn't care what they ordered so he folded up his menu and handed it to the waiter.

"Okay, I'll have that right out for you." The waiter took the now unnecessary menus in one hand and with the other, grabbed two straws from his black apron and slid them across the table. "Let me know if I can get anything else for you." He walked away on a mission to satisfy two more customers. After taking a drink of her water, Nikki carried on the conversation which she couldn't seem to get over.

"Haven't you had a promotion?"

Stad turned his gaze from the ceiling in the corner of the room to his date across the table. "A few actually, but I've been in it much longer so I don't think it's fair to compare our situations." Stad remembered back to what his official story was supposed to be and it was something along the lines of a promotion every three years, but he didn't want to get into too many details.

"Yeah, I guess you're right."

"Don't be so hard on yourself. Enjoy the night."

"I know, sometimes I just get depressed about my job."

"It happens to everybody." Stad thought back to all the long nights spent researching jobs for Max. Hours upon hours, hunched over reading materials that were 90 percent useless and calling up his supplier at all hours of the day, always watching his back and covering his tracks. The more he thought about it the more depressed he got.

The Vivacious Veggie pizza came and went and Nikki and Stad rushed over to the movie theater. The teenager behind the counter rattled off the price as if she had done it thousands of times before. With no hesitation Nikki grabbed money from her purse and exchanged it for tickets.

"You don't have to pay," Stad said.

"You don't either, you covered dinner. I still have that extra buck too, remember?" Nikki smiled and they headed for the entrance. Nikki handed the tickets to the second teenager guarding the entrance.

"Theater six on the right please enjoy the show." His monotonous, expressionless voice contradicted any sort of feelings his statement was trying to invoke. Nikki and Stad locked eyes and tried to hold back laughter.

Theater six was filled with people so they settled for the second row behind a group of children who were well under the age limit for an R rated movie. The trailers had already started, so they fumbled past an entire row of people to squeeze into their seats.

***

"What'd you think?" Stad asked. The night was chilly and they picked up their pace back to Stad's car.

"I thought it was good. I really liked the effects."

"Hollywood magic." Stad shrugged. "I still can't believe you like movies like that. Are you sure you're not just playing along to get on my good side?"

"I swear, I'm a movie buff, I told you. My father used to work for a movie chain so I kind of grew up around it."

"You mean your dad was the guy getting popcorn and tearing tickets?" Stad started to laugh.

"No, no. He wasn't in the theaters, he was a corporate man. He's retired now but my brother practically rode his coattails all the way in. I guess he's one of the top dogs with the corner office and everything."

"Impressive," Stad said while not being impressed.

"Yeah well not for family reunions. He likes to brag about it a lot. He's what a lot of people would call an 'a-hole.' But you know he's still my brother."

"I know some people like that but I'm sure it's different when it's your own family."

"Yeah…" She trailed off and there was a brief moment of silence. "So I was thinking," Nikki said before they reached the car, "since you got to see my place it would only be fair for me to see yours."

"Yeah, sure."

"Great."

"I have to warn you though, it's not nearly as clean as yours."

"That's all right, I know I'm a clean freak. I don't expect many other people can live up to that."

"Don't you need your car though?" Stad asked.

"I'll just pick it up in the morning, it's not that far."

Stad could sense that she just wanted to get back to his place. He tried not to speed all the way back.

When they got there Stad fumbled in his pocket for his keys as Nikki stood next to him smelling like sweet strawberry perfume. He finally found the key to let them in and he swung open the door to let her walk in first.

"Wow." Nikki was attracted to the large window overlooking the skyline. She walked straight past everything else. "Stad, this is amazing."

The city at night was like nothing else. The lighting on the buildings was dramatic and sharp, cutting corners and revealing details that went unseen during the day. The light bounced off the pavement and illuminated hidden crevices and forgotten spaces. Everything made for a beautiful silhouette.

"I would kill for a place like this." She kept walking toward the window until her face was almost pressed up against the glass. Stad tossed his keys on the kitchen counter and Nikki turned around and took notice of the rest of the apartment.

"Mind if I use your bathroom?"

"Go ahead," Stad replied. "It's the door on the left at the end of the hallway." He stared at her butt in her tight jeans as she walked down the hallway. He headed back to the window as she went out of sight.

After a few moments of admiring the skyscrapers, the bathroom door opened and Stad listened to Nikki creeping back toward the living room. When he sensed her at the end of the hallway he turned around and saw her standing at the edge of the living room in her black panties and matching bra.

"Care for any dessert?" She put her hand up and made a "Follow me" motion with her fingers. She turned around and headed for the bedroom. Stad decided her ass looked much better without the jeans.

27

Stad woke with the scent of strawberries in the air. Nikki was sprawled out on more than half of the bed. He reached over for his cell phone and hit the side button to bring the screen to life. It was still early yet, only six, so he decided to try and not wake her. He wriggled himself free, crossed the room and opened the door. He could still hear her sleeping so he pulled the door shut until he heard the click of the bolt slide back into place.

He walked over to the kitchen in his red boxers that he didn't remember putting on in the middle of the night and grabbed a bottle of water from the fridge. He walked over to the window and watched the city life in the morning. The sun was still rising off in the distance and it provided a warm glow to the streets and buildings below. A few cars sputtered here and there, a couple of birds were perched on ledges and a few pedestrians waited for the little man to turn white before crossing. He drank his water and watched the city until the entire sun was visible above the skyline.

"Good morning," Nikki called out from the hall.

"Hey." He turned around and saw her standing in a shirt he must have given her last night. "You're up, good morning."

"Last night was fun." She walked to him, grabbed him by his sides and pulled him in close to give him a gentle kiss.

"Best night I've had in a long time," Stad said with a smirk. He couldn't tell if it was weird to say because he had never said anything like that before or because it was actually the truth. She kissed him again.

"Water?" he asked as he inched away from her. Without saying anything she took the bottle and took a quick sip.

"Thanks, I can't stay too long though, I've got to get to work pretty soon."

"No problem, I was going to put on some coffee if you want any."

"Thanks, but I think I'm just going to freshen up a bit and then head out."

"Do you want a ride to your car or anything?"

"I'm fine. Thanks though." Before Stad could reply she retreated into the bathroom.

Nikki got ready and Stad made some coffee for himself and finished his bottle of water. When it was empty he stared at it and hoped to get inspired for his job, but when nothing came to him he tossed it in the trash.

"Smells good out here." Nikki emerged from the hallway in last night's outfit.

"Sure you don't want any?" Stad asked again.

"Yeah, I'll catch some next time." Nikki headed for the door and Stad followed, coffee mug in hand. "Call me," she said as she stepped outside. Stad stood in the doorway and watched her walk down the hallway toward the elevator.

28

It had been over a week since his date with Nikki and he had intended to call her, but he got sidetracked by his job and now his bleary eyes tried to refocus on his screen.

He pulled up some of the documents from previous sessions and after analyzing the facts and reading some more he decided the best route to take would be the contamination approach. The same approach used for the Tylenol scare wouldn't work anymore since every industry had improved safety implementations dramatically. Now if a soccer mom bought anything with a label even partially scratched, let alone a broken seal, she would be just as likely to call the FBI as she would be to throw it away. He knew the only approach that had a chance for success would be an inside job, which amplified the risk factor yet again.

He pulled up his usual documentation and searched for anything he could find about the process involved with bottling. He spent hours tracking down the companies that specialized in it and the machinery they used, pulling up machine specifications, order forms, policies and even safety training materials.

What he found was that most of the companies bottled their water at a central plant so the same place that bottled the soda drinks, sports drinks and juice drinks also bottled the water. All of the companies manufacture their own bottles and when they arrive at the bottling plan they're sterilized seconds before being put into the chain to be filled.

It was a solid system from end to end and it would be tough to contaminate only one item in a low enough quantity. Another problem was that the actual filler used for the water was also used by all of the other products, so attacking that feature risked the possibility of contaminating soda supplies which were off-limits for this job. Max wouldn't be happy about a voided contract and a hit man looking for them.

After more hours spent looking over repetitive and boring reports, Stad wandered over to the kitchen and opened the fridge, hoping for something quick, easy and light for a late night dinner. He pulled out some leftover spaghetti and threw it in the microwave. As the noodles were heating up he went back to the fridge and debated between water, milk or beer with his meal. He settled on the water bottle shoved in the back corner and hoped it would provide some inspiration.

The microwaved dinged, the fridge shut and in a few short moments he was back in front of his screen looking for more information with a steaming pile of meatballs on his desk. He pulled up some filler machine specs and double checked the information listed to be sure he hadn't missed any glaring holes or gaps that he could sneak a contamination into. He verified that he was right the first time and pulled up specs for all the other machines used in the process from conveyer belts to packaging. It wouldn't help much, but he was trying to grasp onto anything he could.

His research confirmed what his instincts already knew. None of the machines had a vulnerability he could exploit. Even if he had found one he wasn't sure he could make it work in the first place. In the past he had worked with his supplier on setting up a third party, or an insider if the job required one. He was good and prompt with it and didn't provide Stad with any of the details to maintain plausible deniability, but it was a risk Stad was never happy to take. To avoid having to go that route Stad screened all of the currently known employees at the plant for past criminal offenses but because there were so few employees on the ground anymore (most being replaced by automated machinery) the pickings were few and no one seemed like a viable candidate.

He leaned back in his chair as he chomped on his now cold spaghetti. He grabbed his water bottle to wash it down. He tried to twist the cap back on but his carelessness caused him to miss the threads and the cap went flying onto the floor. His eyes followed the noise to the cap's final resting place. He went to pick it up and an idea flew into his head so fast it almost knocked him over.

Stad pulled up all his previous files and re-read about the machines and bottling process in general but couldn't find anything specific about the caps. He had to dig a little deeper but by the end of his spaghetti he was able to track some information down. A lot of the caps were manufactured at the same plant as the bottles, but a few companies outsourced that job to a location in Kentucky. There were three major bottled water companies using this manufacturer, which meant they all used the same caps. This made it much easier to spread out the targets, distract focus and add doubt into the public's mind. Usually if a job focused too much on one player, they are the only ones to suffer while their competition picked up new clients, like the Tylenol scare. Since this job had to target an entire industry, a diversified attack was needed and with this new information, he knew all that hard work was already being done behind the scenes.

He leaned back in his chair and went over possible implementations now that he had identified a weakness. After soaking in all the relevant information he reached for his phone and dialed out to his supplier. He expected a lengthy conversation and waited as the phone rang.

29

Stad woke up startled by the sound of his phone buzzing against his desk. It was moving around and ready to fall off when he reached for it. The alarm had been set for 1:00 AM.

He shut it off and looked around with his eyes half open, the computer screen too bright for him to open them all the way. On the floor was a bottle of whiskey, an empty shot glass and a water bottle next to a stack of messy papers. The printer light was flashing and there was a small catalogs worth of paper hanging off the document tray.

Over time his eyes became accustomed to the glow of the monitor which was displaying information about CEO biographies and information on their backgrounds. One of them had had an affair a couple of years ago with a worker in a bottling plant halfway across the country and another executive had an illegitimate child with his secretary.

Sitting underneath his cellphone on his desk was a childish drawing of a map of the board members for each company and their connections with other companies. There were two names circled in red but he couldn't remember why he had circled them. He scanned the scribbling in the margin but was still stumped. There were more notes jotted down on pieces of paper scattered all over his desk. Some were about contacts within the companies and others were about chemical manufacturers all over the world. In those notes, also highlighted with a red pen were the words chlorine, nicotine, and bromine.

Stad felt dizzy when he got up, so he stood for a while and cracked his knuckles, back and neck before making his way to the living room. He stood at his window and stared across at the tallest skyscraper. Why were the lights on this late into the night? He thought about the notes sitting on his desk and late night romps with secretaries skipped across his mind.

He first noticed the rain as a few drops flew by his window, then, like jumping into a pool after only dipping your toes in, it began to downpour. He stayed at the window as the lightning and thunder show began, lighting up the towering buildings and outlining them against the clouds that had gathered.

The lightning came and went but the storm was still raging on. He left his window and crossed the room to make a pot of coffee. He flicked it on and leaned against the counter. He thought about Nikki and felt bad for never calling her. It was against all of his self-imposed rules and better judgment, but he vowed he would call her the next day.

The smell of brewed coffee began to overtake the stench of the apartment so Stad grabbed the pot and poured some into a complimentary mug that his apartment had come with. Considering the price of the place the mug wasn't the greatest gift and was probably, in all actuality, the most expensive mug he owned.

The storm continued to wash away the dirt and grime the city had gathered throughout the day and Stad listened to the rain hammer against the window. He walked back to his office, picked up his phone and set an alarm for 7:00.

30

Stad stepped off the plane into the warm climate of the southeast. Winter was being phased out at home, but here in Atlanta it had never started.

He weaved his way through the crowds and found the entrance to the train that would take him all the way to his supplier's place. The train rattled its way down the track all the way to the heart of downtown where Stad hopped out and transferred to another train heading west. He took the green line until it didn't go any further and made his way to a taxi stand waiting below the rail stop.

Stad had flown to Atlanta many times before to go over details of a job with his supplier and each time it was at a different location. It was a detail that a lot of people overlooked but one of the many things his supplier did that proved his worth to Stad.

The taxi jumped around on the uneven street as it made its way toward the latest meeting place that was revealed to Stad during his lengthy phone conversation with his supplier. Stad reached into the messenger bag he had thrown onto the seat next to him and pulled out a stack of papers and started thumbing through them. The files were used as a decoy and contained no sensitive information, they were just a printout of a lengthy newspaper article about predictions for the future. The decoy was important in setting up plausibility in the minds of people that

Stad came into contact with during the day, it gave them an image of him preparing or informing himself without compromising any classified details. It was also a useful tool to avoid talking to cabbies.

The taxi stopped outside a strip mall populated by dollar stores and abandoned windows, one of which was his supplier's temporary location. Stad paid in cash and headed for the back of the building. The front of the mall was covered with signs for sales, boarded up entrances, broken windows and neon lights and the back was nothing but a wall of doors, evenly spaced from one store to the next. The first door Stad came across was numbered 101, the second door was creatively labeled 102 but had the name of the store below that, "Dollar Discount." Stad was looking for door "B" and that was all he knew. He stopped at 102 and stared down to the opposite end of the row of doors and wished his supplier had given him something to work with. He trudged onto the next door and hoped the numbering system changed to letters. He didn't find door "B" until the second to last door. Stad could see why it was just "B." Someone had tried to cover up the name of the previous tenant and all that remained in stark white paint against the gray color of the metal was an uppercase letter.

He stepped forward, dragging his foot against the gravel and wrapped on the door three times. He stepped back, picking up his feet more this time, and waited. It was a nice day to be standing around outside, but after a minute he started to wonder if he had come to the wrong place. He checked his watch again to make sure he had the right time when he heard the sound of a lock being undone. Moments after the sound stopped the door opened. Standing in the doorframe was a man who had no name. His hair was long and unkempt, almost forming a knot around his head. He was wearing a simple white t-shirt with multiple visible stains, jeans with even more stains and work boots. With the money he was given, Stad was surprised he didn't at least get a haircut. Appearances didn't matter to Stad though, he wasn't one to talk, and the only important thing was the work that went on behind the scenes and the man standing in front of him had never let him down.

"Good to see you again." The man stepped forward and shielded his eyes with one hand and held out the other.

"Got everything?" Stad asked, grasping the man's hand.

"Not even a hello? They're over on that table." He pointed into the dark room where Stad could just make out the outline of a table off in the distance. The two men stepped inside and as the door closed and shut out the sunlight the four dim fluorescent lights in each corner became more apparent.

"Cutting back on the electricity bill?"

"Just like these better."

Stad walked across the room and his eyes adjusted to the change in light source. He started to make out more details and objects in the room, like wooden crates against one wall, what looked like miscellaneous packaging supplies against another and two large containers in the middle of the room, one of which looked to be full of empty water bottles.

"Looks like you've been getting a lot done."

"Well that's what you pay me for isn't it?"

"It's why I keep paying you." Stad reached out for the metal chair against one side of the table and could see that a little sunlight made its way through the wooden boards covering the front windows. "That's what this is for." Stad put his bag on the table, reached in and pulled out stacks of bills. "Your share for those little noisemakers that wreaked havoc on mailboxes across the country."

"Nice. You know I saw a copycat on the news a while back, a month ago, maybe longer, I don't remember. The dumbass blew his hand clean off."

"Well hopefully this money will keep you producing good work and making sure that those aren't my hands getting blown off." Stad watched the man count his money, knowing that some of it was likely to be passed along further. No business partners were ever mentioned but Stad wasn't dumb enough to think his supplier worked alone. Stad was also positive his supplier thought the same thing about him. Both of the men took each other at face value because that's all they could afford in such a high-risk career choice. So far it had worked out well for them, and as the grin on the supplier's face grew larger Stad had a feeling it wouldn't be going downhill anytime soon.

"Nice, you're all square man." The supplier stacked his money back up and walked it over to where the wooden crates were. He came back with a large baggy and some papers. "Here's what I got for you." He dropped the sack on the table and slapped the papers down next to them. "These are your poisoned wafers. Don't go picking them up though. They're technically only dangerous if you ingest them, but its best to wash your hands twice if you touch one. Believe me, I've learned the hard way after all these years. You don't want to be touching poison and then taking a piss or eating a burger."

"They're smaller than I thought they would be."

"This is the best batch to make it out of testing. I outlined everything in there for you." He pointed to the papers that Stad hadn't looked at yet. "Basically one of those guys will disintegrate in less than 30 seconds after making contact with the water and the average timespan was four days for one to dissolve due to evaporation."

"Four days? Shipments are usually on shelves within three."

"Four's just the average. Besides, most people probably let it sit around in their fridge for a while anyway. Even if it doesn't dissolve they're so tiny no one's going to notice, right?" His supplier produced a pair of tweezers from his pocket, opened the bag of wafers and grabbed one.

"That is pretty thin." Stad leaned forward for a better view. It looked like a flat, foggy contact lens. His supplier reached for his feet and kept the wafer above the table for Stad to see. He came back up with a bottle of water.

"This is what I'm talking about, watch this." He dropped the wafer into the bottle, forcing it past the hole in the top. The wafer chipped into pieces and landed in the water less than an inch below. Stad watched as the tiny wafer chunks drifted on the top and became smaller and smaller until he couldn't see them anymore.

"That's pretty impressive."

"It hasn't always been that pretty, but this batch works really nice."

Stad flipped through the rudimentary reports and he could see that these really were the best option. This version of the wafer was the best without crumbling or being too big and bulky to work effectively.

"I've got a guy who I've already set up inside that bottling facility. It'll be pretty simple. He'll bring the machinery down for maintenance and swap out the regular caps for these bad boys."

"You trust him?"

"As much as I trust you."

Good point.

Stad would have preferred to do the job himself but the risk in going out to the field on this one seemed too high. There was a lot of paperwork involved in getting hired and by stepping inside the plant his identity would be captured on multiple cameras. Plus there was always the fact that he couldn't just walk away from a job like that after a major incident and expect it to go unnoticed.

"Then I guess I have to trust him too."

"I also went into some more detail about the effects of the chemical. It was a little tricky to gather all of that, but it's in there. I can trigger the job to start in less than a day whenever I get the word."

"Yeah well, as much as I'd love to, I've got some more waiting to do myself. I expect this one will need to have action taken quickly, so just be prepared."

"I always am."

"I see that." Stad held up the report. "Anything else I need to know right now?"

"What else do you need to know? You practically wrote that report for me. I had so much information it was a piece of cake."

"Sounds like everything's in pretty good shape."

"Like I said, you just say the word and it's on."

"Then I'll be in touch." Stad grabbed the papers, shoved them in his bag which was now almost empty and stood up. "Don't blow all that money either."

"Why not? It'll just get replenished this summer."

"I don't have too many specifics on payment for this one, so don't be counting on it for your retirement fund." Stad laughed.

"Good idea, I'll probably just use it for moving expenses anyway. I've been in this building a little too long."

"Maybe next time you can get a place with lights?" Stad joked.

"Maybe next time you bring a flashlight."

31

The cab pulled up at a drug store not too far away at the corner of a busy intersection. Stad got out and headed for the store. He hoped that cold and flu season wasn't as prevalent in this part of the country so he wouldn't be bothered.

He scanned the aisles and found the medicines near the back and close to the pharmacy counter that seemed to be abandoned at this hour, which worked out well for him. He walked past the cough drops and vitamins to get to the boxed medications. He reached for a box of orange and white cold medicine on one of the higher shelves, flipped it over and began reading and pretending like he was interested in a possible purchase. "May cause drowsiness" was the first warning he saw so he skipped ahead a few words. "Do not operate heavy machinery."

Perfect.

He reached for his familiar marker and covered the words, leaving behind only a slight trace of irregularity on an otherwise clean packaged product. He repeated his actions for the seven remaining boxes before putting the marker back in his pocket.

32

The man in the black suit loosened his tie to prepare to make the biggest proposal in his life. He got to his feet and cleared his throat.

"If we sabotage the movie industry the customers will have no other choice but to flee to their homes and turn their entertainment centers into their personal movie theaters. With this flood back to the market our industry will expand and once the customers are attracted I am certain they will not be able to revert to anything else." His voice carried a tone of importance throughout the room and he had the full attention of Suit #1, sucking on his cigarette.

"How do we go about sabotaging the movie industry?" The leader of the Three Bald Mice asked the question, still red-faced and shaking. The black-suited man slicked his hair back even further with his hand so that it was matted to his scalp.

"I have a few ideas and would like to discuss them further but first let me draw your attention to an earlier plan hatched by this board back in the 90s. The DVD was just becoming a threatening force in the entertainment area and the movie industry fought back by waging legal wars that carried on far too long. In order to bolster DVD sales and create an effect that would harm the theaters in return, a plan was launched to draw attention away from the big screen and put peoples' butts back on the living room couch." He looked toward Suit #1 and the room held its collective breath.

"Is this the HIV needle proposal?" Suit #1 asked. All eyes shifted back to the man at the opposite end of the room.

"You are correct, sir. In a few select theaters across the country needles were placed in chairs, causing a moviegoer to get pricked when they sat down. A note was attached stating that they had been infected with HIV. Of course the needles were not infected and the main point of the proposal was to get patrons out of the theaters and back into their homes buying their own entertainment systems, free of fear from infected needles."

"I thought that didn't work." Mouse #2 spoke up, almost interrupting the man in black who was once again squashing his hair into his head.

"It caused a slight dip in sales that the movie industry recovered from by releasing a couple of blockbusters later in the year. And of course after the needles were tested and shown not to contain the virus, fear subsided and people went flooding back to the theaters. The markets eventually worked themselves into an equilibrium which brings us here today in a similar situation."

"What are your bright ideas this time around?" The lead mouse piped in.

"I would say our first step is to come up with an idea. We know the industry in and out and should be able to put something very powerful together. We also need to contact the company we worked through last time and discuss possible ventures with them. We haven't needed their services in a long time, so information for them is sparse, but we need to get in touch somehow." He paused and looked around the room to nods of approval until he caught the eyes of Suit #1.

"I agree," Suit #1 said. "I just don't want any knowledge of the operation outside of what I've already heard. Do what you have to do." He stood up and towered over the table shrouded in a hazy fog. "I don't want to mess around this time either, we need to deliver a huge blow." He took a puff from his cigarette and exhaled the smoke straight toward the ceiling. "This time we go big."

33

"Number 92," Stad said into the microphone. The door clicked opened and he walked in. Max was standing near the windows overlooking the street below. When he turned to see Stad enter he walked over to his desk and sat in the power position.

"I hope you've got some good stuff for me."

"I think I do." Stad set his materials down and took a seat.

"First off," he started, "you talked about the Tylenol scare of 1992 and in researching this job I came across many similarities. It was a big impact job and no one had previously pulled off anything near its level. Their revenue fell drastically and everyone from our side walked away with a brand new car. I think we can have the same impact with this job, but to achieve that we're going to have to be on the very top of our game." He shoved one of the portfolios in Max's direction. Max snatched it up and peeled back the shiny cover.

"My research indicates that the public started out with a very high suspicion of the industry dating back to 1996. This report details all of the investigations into the industry that have been made since then. The very first, starting in the same year, shows that the CEO of the second largest market share player denied claims that their product was simply local tap water. These same charges were then brought to other CEOs who feverishly denied them. It wasn't until a major investigation in 2000 that a former CEO admitted their product wasn't always what they claimed it to be. This investigation found that there were not one or two companies using plain old tap water, but tens of companies using the same deceptive technique. The graph on page 12 shows the stock value and consumer confidence for these companies for the year before this investigation and the year after the investigation took place."

"Since 2000 there have been smaller examinations over the years but the bottled water industry has fought hard and pushed back against these claims to not only hide them, but in some cases try to reverse what they were saying. Some have gone as far as saying products now contain 'enhanced nutrients' and are much better for you. While a select few of these products actually do contain some added benefits, most are marketing fluff. Time and time again these corporations brush off attacks and push them out of the public eye, which leads us to where we are today, with an industry on the rise and demand at an all-time high."

"That's great, Stad." Max closed the report and tossed it back on the desk. "But what's that got to do with what we're trying to accomplish?"

"I'm just trying to build a case for why I think this plan will work. As already pointed out, the public is suspicious of the industry even if they aren't aware of it. To take advantage of this all we'll need is one slipup and we can expect to see a similar decline compared to the one in 2000."

"Okay, so what is that one small slipup?" Max interjected.

"We're going to poison the water." Stad reached for another repot and handed it over to his boss. "This outlines how we are going to do that. In there are details of the chemical manufacturer I have indirect contact with. In working with them

I have found that there is a small amount of bromine in most tap and bottled water. Typically this amount is negligible and doesn't even show in most testing samples. However, if we were to increase that amount we could accomplish an effect that would be perfect for this job. We're looking at extreme sickness, vomiting, diarrhea, fever and all the associated fun stuff. I have been assured that we can have this produced and setup to ship anywhere we need."

"Have we used these chemical guys before?"

"No, but I'm working with them through my usual supplier who I've worked with before. He's been very reliable. He also helped me develop this plan and knows what needs to be accomplished."

"But the chemical manufacturer is a wildcard?" Max picked at his fingertips.

"My supplier has used them in the past and in contacting them he uses company names, fronts, fake addresses and throwaway cell phones. He's good at what he does. I'm sure the chemical manufacturer has limited visibility."

"All right, so what's that buy us? How do we get that contamination done?"

"Luckily for us a lot of the processes behind bottling some of the water are centrally located making it a much easier target. The bottles themselves are out since they're sanitized multiple times and once again right before they are filled. The water was an option at one point but it would require much more volume of chemicals and the tanks where the water is stored are infamous for being difficult to breach, for obvious reasons. After eliminating both of those options we're left with only one feasible choice, the cap. There are three major companies that use one separate manufacturing plant for their water bottle caps. The caps are made in that plant then shipped out to be used in the bottling process. In all of the cases for these three companies the caps arrive in shrink wrap and are dumped into a large bin immediately to cap the bottles."

"I must be missing something." Max shifted his lean from left to right. "How does contaminating the caps help at all?"

"The bromine is being made into a paper-thin wafer." Stad tossed more papers in Max's direction. "Specs are outlined in front of you. This wafer is fitted into the bottom of the cap and thin enough to go unnoticed by a casual observer. For the contamination we have a two stage setup. The primary objective is to drop the wafer into the water upon being capped on the bottle. When the capper machine screws on the cap, the perforated edge will become separated and let the rest of the wafer fall into the water and dissolve within 30 seconds. The backup system is a failsafe. If the wafer gets stuck in the cap, I estimated that over time while the bottle's in transit, evaporation will cause cracks in the wafer and allow some portions to fall into the water. I anticipate that this would happen no more than one percent of the time. My supplier has a contact that will be able to pull off this inside job at the central cap manufacturing plant, so exposure isn't a problem for us either." Stad produced another report and slid it across the desk. Max moved some papers around to make room for the new information.

"Inside that report is the plan for national distribution. I calculated around 30,000 total units spread across the three central companies. If dispersed properly from the internal plant then our product should be distributed throughout the nation. Starting on page 50 is a detailed analysis of expected stock decrease, impact to CEO payout and company performance as well as expected reaction from consumers and fallout from around the industry and others involved. There is also a report on the expected investigation afterwards and the results that should lead nowhere, most likely blaming the entire issue on the water source."

Stad breathed out a heavy sigh and sat and watched Max flip through pages and waited for him to point out some flaw in the plan. Max furrowed his brow at some pages, pressed his fingers to his lips on others and sometimes had no discernable expression on his face at all. Stad sipped on water from a glass in front of him and watched Max switch papers.

"I like it," Max finally said after closing the final report. "I like all of it."

"Great, that's what I was hoping to hear."

"I don't really think they're going to find much to disapprove of."

"I hope so." The "they" he was referring to were the people who had contacted Max in the first place, the people working for the soda industry. Stad never met them or knew who they were, but he didn't care as long as their checks cleared.

"Let's not get ahead of ourselves though Stad, I still have to present this to them, so until then let's just lay low and hope they sign off on it. I can call you tomorrow after the presentation but don't expect too much on it right away, they like to take their time with stuff."

"Don't worry about calling. How long do you think they'll need?"

"Hard to say. You know how it is though, they want us to do everything in a matter of days and then when it's on them they don't get back to us for weeks, maybe months. My gut tells me it won't take that long on this job, but I'd expect at least a week or two before they make a final decision."

"I'll try to keep myself busy until then."

"Just keep yourself out of the spotlight, all right?" Max stood up and Stad was quick to follow.

"You need anything else from me right now?" Stad asked as he started to head for the door.

"I think I've got all I can handle." Max shifted his gaze down to the new pile of paperwork scattered across his desk. "I'll review and let you know if I need anything else before the presentation."

34

It wasn't like he was trying to avoid her, he actually enjoyed being with her, it was just that he had gotten so busy with the bottled water job he had put her in the back of his mind and she never managed to surface to the top. He was having a hard time trying to find space in his life to fit her in. His typical relationships never lasted past the first night and he didn't mind, he liked his own time and doing his own thing. Nikki had somehow managed to surpass that one night and turn it into two. Stad wouldn't be upset if it had stopped at one above the normal, but he was more excited than he expected when he heard her voice and caught a scent of her strawberry perfume coming from behind him.

"Why is it that every time I tell you to call me, you never do?"

"Nikki, hey." Stad turned around in his stool, drink still in hand.

"Are you just trying to avoid me?" She walked to the empty spot next to Stad's barstool.

"No, sorry. My life has just been kind of crazy right now, that's all. I didn't want you to get caught up in all of it. Besides," he continued without taking a breath and giving her the chance to jump in, "you seem to find a way to get in touch with me all the time, what are you doing here? I thought you didn't like this place."

"I never said that."

"Get you anything to drink ma'am?" Jones approached the new customer.

"No, I better not. Thanks though."

"Let me know if you change your mind." Jones walked away.

"You come all the way here and don't even order a drink?" Stad asked and watched Jones scuttle away. He knew the old man was listening from the other end of the bar.

"I'm on the job, I've got a showing in a little bit not too far from here and it would be really bad for business to show up smelling like alcohol."

"So what, you just wanted to stop by and relax a little before that?" Stad leaned against the bar and tried to figure out if she was telling the truth.

"I had some time to kill between showings. Since I was around I thought I'd swing by, somehow I knew you'd be here."

"So what you're saying is that you're stalking me?"

"If I was stalking you, I'd be 100 percent sure that you were here, I was only around 85." She laughed and curled a wild strand of hair behind her ear.

"Congratulations then, you found me."

"And I can see that crazy life isn't enough to keep you from your favorite bar."

"I've just got enough downtime to savor my favorite drink and listen to some good jazz."

"Sorry to hear that," Nikki said. "I can leave you alone if you want."

"No, you're fine. Like I said, you caught me in a moment of downtime." Stad knew it would be a hard lie to keep up with since now that he had presented the job to Max he had nothing but time to kill until he heard back from him.

"You got big clients keeping you chained to your desk or something?"

"Just everything at work has kind of been out of sorts. I had to fly down to-" Stad pretended like he had to clear his throat and caught himself almost saying Atlanta. "...Texas earlier in the week and I think I'm going back but it'll probably be a last-minute decision. Things are just really hectic."

"Why do they need you down in Texas?"

"It's a big takeover and they just feel more comfortable with someone on-site, double checking all the numbers and making sure the books are in order so they can have better estimates on costs and everything."

"That sucks."

"Yeah, I think it's stupid considering I could do the exact same thing from my office here but you'd be surprised at how many companies request to have someone on-site." Stad took a drink.

"Travel is nice though, and you get to see places for free. That's definitely not a perk everyone has."

"Yeah, I guess they can't have you selling houses in other states, huh?"

"That would be a little bit of a challenge." She laughed again and the loose strand of hair fell back in front of her face.

"I don't want to drag you down with me, how are things going for you? You're still doing showings I see, so that's good, right? Have you gotten that promotion yet?" Stad lifted his glass back to his lips.

"No promotion, but it's definitely been getting busier for us. Now that spring is here people are putting their homes up for sale and everyone is out looking. It's pretty rare that I have two separate showings like I do tonight. I can't really complain though, I'd rather be busy than have nothing to do and be worried about losing my job all the time."

"Yeah." Stad had no idea how that felt. Ever since Max had brought him on board years ago Stad had no worries of being fired. Leaving a company like his, voluntarily or not, was as rare as an albino zebra. Only a few people he knew had managed to leave and it was a big deal that took way longer than it should have.

"Speaking of work," Nikki said, "I had better get going. I want to get there a little early to make sure everything is set up. Are you busy at all this weekend?"

"Honestly, I have no idea. I could be, I may not be. Like I said, with all the changes going on I won't know until the last possible minute."

"Well I hate to tell you to call me if you're free, because we both know how well that works out."

"I'll try to remember to let you know, but I can't make any promises. How's that?"

"I think I can make that work. But if I come back here and find you sitting on that same stool…" She stood up and flung her hair back again. "You do still have my number, right?"

"Of course."

"All right, if I don't see you then good luck with your number crunching. I hope that deal finally goes through so you have some more free time."

"You and me both. Good luck yourself." Stad watched her leave as her strawberry aroma faded away.

35

After a few nights of drinking and not hearing anything back from Max, Stad reached out for his cell phone and dialed Nikki's number.

"Hello?" Her voice sounded soothing over the phone.

"Nikki, it's Stad." He heard no response. He was sure she was there from the breathing he could hear over the line. He waited a few moments before clearing his throat. "Nikki? You there?"

"Yeah," she finally chimed in. "I'm here, I'm just so shocked that you're calling that I'm having troubles speaking."

"Very funny."

"Sorry, I just couldn't help it. What's going on?"

"Well that's just it, I told you I'd call you and here's that call."

"I'm glad you finally had enough free time in your life to remember that I exist. I take it that means you're free this weekend?"

"I am." The words poured out of his mouth and he was relieved that he no longer had to lie.

"So do you want to get together?"

"Sure." His words were followed by nothing. All he could hear was breathing again.

"What did you have in mind?" Nikki's voice broke the silence.

"I don't know, I'm just giving you a call because you wanted me to. Do you have anything you want to do?"

"Actually, if you don't have anything specific I know of something. I've always wanted to go but before I moved I was always too far away and not really up to drive that much."

"What is it?" Stad spoke as Nikki paused to take a breath.

"It's a free event at the contemporary art museum downtown."

"Well, that's not really the type of thing I'm into."

"They're serving free appetizers," she said.

"You should have mentioned that sooner. I'll go anywhere there's free food."

"Great, it starts at six. Since you live much closer I thought I'd meet you at your place?"

"You mean in two hours?" Stad asked, glancing at the clock.

"Is that okay?"

"Yeah, whatever works. Like I said, I'm a free man this weekend."

"Okay, I'll try to be at your place a little early."

"I won't get my hopes too high, but I'll see you then."
Stad hung up and was now focused on how he was going to cope with being in an art museum for a night. He didn't have too much time to think about it and the two hours disappeared faster than expected. Two heavy thuds landed on his front door at 5:55. He opened the door and saw Nikki leaning against the jamb in a sleek black dress, sharp red heels and a diamond necklace hugging her bust and falling just above her neckline.

"Wow." He once again felt outclassed in his five-year-old sport coat and matching pants. "You need anything? Water?

Wine?" Stad started backing away from the door but kept his eyes on her the whole time.

"I'm okay, but can I use your bathroom?"

"Of course. You know where it is."

"Thanks." She headed down the hall. Stad was hoping she would reappear like last time, but when she came back into the living room fully clothed he realized he would have to wait for that to happen again.

"Ready to head out?" Nikki asked.

"Yep." Stad held the door open for her and they started walking down the hallway. When they reached the elevators they stepped inside and Stad looked at the lights above the doors, watching them count backward and getting closer to one.

"Are you secretly an alcoholic, Stad?" Nikki blurted out.

"What?" he asked.

"It's just that you seem to be at Jones' all the time."

"I really like the music." Stad could see the look of concern on her face. "Plus it's just a nice place to unwind and let things off my chest. Jones is like my cheap psychiatrist."

"Or, with enough drinks, a very expensive one."

"Never thought of it that way." Stad shrugged.

"What do you guys talk about?"

"I'm afraid I can't divulge that." He smirked. "You know, client bartender confidentiality."

"Oh yeah, how could I forget?"

"Are you trying to tell me that you don't have a place like that? A place you can just go and put out everything that's on your mind? I'm sure work stresses you out too."

"Of course it does, but I have a few hobbies that help distract me and take me away for a while."

"Well as long as you have something. I can just imagine with a new job and everything that it's pretty rough."

"Am I getting a free psychiatrist session today?" There was a hint of laughter in her voice.

"You can take my advice or not, I'm just putting it out there."

"I know, I'm sorry," Nikki said. The numbers above the doors switched to letters and now showed "L." The elevator opened and the two stepped out and began to walk across the lobby. "I don't want to discourage you or make it seem like I don't care, because I really do."

"I know, and it's all right, you know I don't get offended easily."

"I know, it only happened once back in the 80s, right?" Nikki laughed and her heels clicked against the floor until they hit the concrete outside.

"You can wait here and I'll pull the car around." Stad started walking away from his date.

"Actually," she raised her voice so Stad would hear her, "I thought we'd walk."

"You sure? I can't imagine walking all that way in those heels is the best feeling."

"I can manage. Plus it's a nice night out and it's not that far anyway."

"All right, but I'm not carrying you back." They both laughed and started walking down the street in the direction of the museum.

36

Spotlights drenched the rectangular columns that lined the front entrance of the museum. Stad and Nikki stepped inside to the sounds of techno music and a whiny voice.

"Welcome to the Moderno Showing." A lady dressed in all white appeared from off the side of the doors. "Refreshments are straight ahead and the gallery begins just beyond that. If you have any questions please contact an event specialist located throughout the gallery."

Stad tried to keep moving forward but he found Nikki's hand clasping his to hold him back.

"Thanks." Nikki stopped near the woman. "Can you tell me where the restrooms are?"

"Just beyond that hallway." The lady in white pointed out into the distance and Nikki turned to look while Stad eyed the refreshments in the opposite direction.

"Thanks, I'll be right back." She dropped Stad's hand and headed in the direction the woman had pointed.

Stad cruised over to the refreshment bar that consisted of small glasses of wine, no bigger than shot glasses, all different kinds of cheeses, special crackers, a vegetable tray and a mysterious meat-like substance. With nothing else in sight he picked up a couple of boring looking crackers and one of the glasses of red wine. He circled the room he was in while trying to catch glimpses of the gallery beyond. He couldn't see much from his vantage point other than what appeared to be a giant skull. He rolled his eyes and threw back his tiny glass of wine and started heading back to grab another when Nikki came up to his side.

"Getting started without me?" she asked.

"You gave me no choice." He scooped up two glasses and gave one to his date.

"How is it?"

"Dry. You ready to check out this weird crap?"

"Be nice Stad, somebody worked hard on all of this."

"Washing machines work hard too." They walked toward a room with paintings spread out on the wall. "What's that one saying? 'One man's treasure is another man's trash'?"

"It's the other way around," Nikki replied.

"Whatever." Stad looked at the painting in front of him, it was a giant giraffe and elephant hybrid animal.

"You don't think that is at least a little interesting?" Nikki asked.

"I don't know, I guess I don't get it. It's called 'Strongility.' What does that mean?"

"Well I'm assuming it's a combination of strong and agile, or something like that, with the elephant representing the strong portion of the painting and the giraffe signifying agility."

"Giraffes are agile?" Stad continued to stare, puzzled by the image.

"I have no idea, but you have to at least admit that it's painted very well."

"Yeah, it's pretty good. I mean, I know I couldn't do something like that." Stad kept moving along the wall and headed for the second painting while finishing off his second tiny wine glass. The title was "Flexuborness."

"Well see," Stad said, turning to Nikki who followed him over, "this one doesn't even sound like a real word, it's just a stretch."

"What would you have called it then?"

"I wouldn't have called it anything. In fact, I would have never painted it in the first place."

"Maybe you're just not a creative person."

"I guess not. Do you want any more to drink?"

"I'll take another if you're offering." Nikki handed her empty glass to Stad who turned heel and marched back to the bar area. After refilling, he snuck back up to Nikki who had moved on to a painting of a buffalo rhinoceros.

"Do you think any of these are good?" Stad whispered.

"I think this one is interesting."

"I didn't ask if you thought they were interesting."

"They're painted well, they're just not really my taste though." Nikki grabbed her new wine glass and took a sip. They rounded the corner and entered a separate area filled with statues of various items, including the giant skull which Stad had spotted earlier from the refreshment stand. They walked closer and discovered that the giant skull was made up of a bunch of smaller skulls stacked on top of one another.

"Hm." They stood and stared at it for a while and tried to soak up the deeper meaning that the artist must have been trying to get through.

"I like it," Stad said after failing to get any such meaning.

"Not my style." Nikki walked over to the next statue.

"So I'm guessing you don't like this one either?" Stad asked. They were standing in front of a life size horse riding a human.

"How'd you know? What do you say we speed this thing up?"

"I'm okay with that, I already had the food I came here for anyway." They continued following the wooden floor into another room which was full of piles of trash shaped to look like other objects. The trash room carried on into finger paintings of severed fingers which led them to a room full of various coffee beans on fire which turned into a room containing nothing but cotton balls, clothes hangers and sticky notes which was not to be confused with the room full of trash.

"I thought I was confused before, but now I'm not even sure I know what this place is." Stad turned to Nikki with a sixth empty wine glass in his hand.

"I can't help you there," Nikki replied after only her third glass.

"How many more rooms are there?" Stad looked toward the end of the current room and saw a sign pointing forward leading to an exhibit titled "Fear," which meant there was at least one more, which was one too many.

"Yeah, I don't think I want to stay to find out if I like the rest or not," Nikki said. "Let's get out of here." They passed the refreshment table and found a spot to put their empty glasses. They reached the entrance and the hostess stepped forward with a white smile to match her outfit.

"Thank you for enjoying the show." She turned as the couple whizzed by her. "Please tell your friends, and remember we are open every other-" The door slammed before the rest of her marketing pitch could make it out.

After escaping the crazy house they decided that the dry crackers hadn't fulfilled either of them, so they headed to the nearest café. It was a place called "Linwood" not too far down the street. Most of the seats were empty and they chose a cozy table in the corner.

"If you absolutely had to choose a favorite piece of art, what would it be?" Stad asked, seated across from Nikki.

"Probably the room full of coffee beans. At least it smelled good." She glanced above her menu. "What about you?"

"The giant skull made of little skulls, easy."

"Really? I thought it was kind of creepy, way too much darkness and death for me."

"You mean the whole exhibit didn't give you that vibe? What sort of god creates a tortured hybrid mutant lizard bird? And those severed fingers smeared in rainbow colors, the room full of trash and all that fire?"

"Sorry, I've blocked it all out. All I can think about now is the smell of that coffee." Nikki closed her eyes and breathed in loud enough for Stad to hear.

"I guess." He ignored her breathing patterns. "I wasn't impressed, but I'm sure there were lots of people who were."

"To each his own. I bet a lot of people would find my job and hobbies boring, but I don't care what they think."

"What are your hobbies anyway?" Stad cut in. "You mentioned them earlier but I forgot to ask about them."

"I collect stuff." She looked down at the table and started to fidget with her napkin.

"What kind of stuff?" Stad prodded. He watched her fold back the corners of her napkin and could tell he had struck a nerve. It was payback, he had to suffer through the art museum and now it was her turn. After a long silence, she finally answered.

"I collect leaves."

"Leaves?" Stad emphasized. "As in, from trees?"

"Yep…"

"Is this the part where you tell me that you used to be in a mental hospital?"

"Hey." She darted her eyes toward Stad. "You don't have to be so mean about it."

"I'm just giving you a hard time."

"I just think some of them are really neat looking." Nikki lowered her voice as the waitress returned and took their orders. Stad waited until the waitress was well out of earshot before speaking up again.

"Leaves? Really?"

"Okay, I get it, I have a weird hobby. Make fun of me all you want but I like it. I'm sure you have something just as embarrassing."

"Why would you assume that?"

"Am I wrong?"

"Not really." He took a drink of his water and looked around the room.

"Oh come on, you're not going to tell me?" Nikki crossed her arms. "I shared my leaf collection with you, that's got to be worth something."

"Okay, I do have something that's a little different."

"That's a start. Is it a collection of stuffed teddy bears or butterfly statues or something?"

"It's not that different. I'll just show you sometime."

"I think I've seen a horror movie with this premise. Some guy takes his date back to his house to 'show her something' and she ends up being another collectible stuffed underneath the house."

"If it makes you feel any better," Stad interjected, "I think it's against the lease to bury bodies underneath my complex."

"Not really helping, Stad. For all I know you could own an empty field or abandoned warehouse somewhere."

"You're getting warmer." Stad laughed at his own joke but saw that Nikki was a little more concerned. "You don't have to worry about it, I promise."

"All right." She uncrossed her arms. "As long as you promise to show me at some point."

Their meals came and went just as quickly as they had arrived. At one point Nikki and Stad tried to draw their own animal hybrids on the napkins, but in the end they both turned out looking like dogs. They stayed in their corner table until the wait staff started putting chairs on top of tables. Stad left a hefty tip and he and Nikki stepped out into the tepid springtime air to begin their walk back home.

When they reached Stad's apartment the elevator took them up and Nikki raced ahead to wait at his door. She grabbed the top of the frame with one hand and the opposite side with the other and shifted her hips just enough to show off her curves. Stad saw one eye peering through the dark brown strands of hair that dangled in front of her face.

"What took you so long?" she whispered. Stad stretched his keys for the door and kissed her. He turned the handle and they both fell inside.

37

"We desperately need to drive people out of movie theaters and back onto their couches. Once this happens, they'll have no other option but to buy our systems. Upgrades will be the next hot ticket and it'll get them even more hooked. They won't be going back to the theaters." The man in the black suit was leading the discussion after the departure of Suit #1 and his blonde assistant.

"How are we supposed to guarantee that?" A voice came from the middle of the table.

"We can't, but if we go drastic enough I know we'll be successful. Just put yourself in the position of a customer and ask yourself what you would want your family to do if something disastrous happened in a movie theater. Would you want to go back? We have to strike during the summer blockbusters and make the biggest impact and reach the most people."

"Like if all the movie theater popcorn was poisoned?" Another anonymous voice spoke up.

"Exactly!" The man in the black suit snapped his fingers. "Just like that. What else?" There were murmurs from the men at the table as the man in black paced.

"Seizure-inducing films!" Another voice from the crowd.

"That would be a challenge but I like where you're taking it. That's the right direction, something big, something noticeable, something dangerous."

"Tear gas!" Another shout from the table.

"Electrifying seats!"

"Subliminal messages!"

"Exploding candy!"

"All right, okay, calm down for a minute. I think we might be getting a little off track here. Stay focused on something big, we need to think bigger here. Something that would send a shock through every chain in America. Something that would drive people away, make them scared, make it so they would never want to go back." The man circled the table.

"Maybe the company we reach out to will have an idea."

"I think we know the industry better than them, don't we?" The man in the black suit stopped and made eye contact with everyone before continuing. "I think we're all capable of coming up with a superior plan."

The bubbling excitement in the room subsided after the man in the black suit challenged the other suits. Now eyes just wandered in silence. Some started to look up for inspiration, others looked down and the man leading the group closed his eyes. The silence was intense and the thinking almost became audible. It had become a room full of ghosts in expensive suits. After everyone had become a little older, one of them spoke.

"I remember a while back everyone was scared shitless about anthrax and explosives. Couldn't we do something like that?" The room shook their collective heads and turned into one giant yes man. The black-suited man was standing at the head of the table and folded his hands in the church steeple position, resting near his mouth. His eyes were closed and the proposed solution was chugging through his mind. The room waited for his thoughts.

"Gentlemen," he announced, "I appreciate your feedback greatly but believe I've come up with a perfect solution." There were whispers from the table as the men began questioning why the anthrax and explosives idea was pushed to the side. The whispers stopped when the man in the black suit cleared his throat. "How does everyone feel about guns?"

38

Stad sat on his couch, sipped coffee and felt guilty that he couldn't share more of his real life with Nikki. She was different than the other women he was used to bringing home and now that he had shared multiple nights with her she was becoming part of his somewhat normal routine. He wasn't quite sure yet if that was a good thing or not. He got up and stood at the window. Were things changing? Were they supposed to?

His cell phone rang and before he answered he glanced at the screen and saw that it was Max.

"Yeah?"

"Stad, it's Max. Can you swing by the office today?"

"Good morning to you too."

"Sorry, it's been a long couple of days."

"I hope you're calling to give me good news."

"Yeah I've just got to run a few things by you real quick." Max didn't even pause for a breath between the end of Stad's sentence and the beginning of his own.

"Is everything all right?"

"Yeah, yeah. I just need you in here today, sound good?"

"Sure."

"That'd be great. Thanks." Max hung up without saying anything else and left Stad to wonder what it was all about. Although more concerned than usual, Stad took his time showering and getting ready before heading out to meet his boss.

The early morning traffic was light and Stad made good time getting to the familiar giant building. The passphrase let him into Max's office where Stad found his boss hunched over his desk studying papers spread out in front of him.

"Have a seat." Max didn't look up as Stad walked in.

"What's this all about?" Stad pulled out the chair and sat down.

"I need to make sure that you're absolutely certain you can move quickly on this water industry job."

"Of course it can move quickly, I've studied that plan inside and out, no doubts in my mind. Why? How'd the presentation go?"

"It went fine." Max wiped some sweat away from his forehead. "I've just been worried because I haven't heard from them since. I expected a response by now but I can't even get in touch with them. I have no way of knowing what they're thinking, when they want it done or even if they like the plan at all. What if they decided to go with one of our competitors?"

"You need to relax, boss. Maybe get some more sleep?"

"I've been trying, I just can't."

"I'm sure they're just taking their time before pulling the trigger. It's a big corporate decision and I'm sure they don't want to just jump into it."

"But I can't give this one over to our competition." Max wiped away even more sweat.

"I know that they wouldn't reach out to anyone else, that plan was rock solid and no one else could come up with anything half as good as that." Stad knew about their competitors but had yet to see any of their work have as big an impact as theirs. Stad worked for the big boys and every other company aspired to be them. There were a lot of people at the firm who had been around for a long time and all the tips and tricks were passed on to him and the other active agents. They had made a reputation for being the best and there were never any disappointments. He knew that after they received his plan, the soda industry wouldn't pursue anybody else.

"Yeah, you're probably right," Max said. "I just haven't been receiving very good news lately so I'm starting to worry."

"What'd you hear?"

"We received a proposal request late last night." Max rested his hands in his lap.

"How's that bad news? Who's the target?" Stad leaned forward, excited at the prospect of a new job. The best part of any job for him was the beginning, the newness of finding out what or who the targets were and the ideas that ran through his mind. He started to think of all sorts of techniques that he could pull. He smiled at the thought of Nikki saying he wasn't creative, if only she knew how creative he actually was.

Max produced a manila folder from underneath his desk and slid it to Stad.

"It's the movie industry," he said.

"Wow." Stad could see why Max thought it was bad news. These guys were a huge target and the job would be a huge risk. Any slipups or small mistakes meant disaster not only for Stad but for the entire firm. The movie industry was notorious for retaliation if anyone ever went against them or caused them any type of harm.

"Who's after those guys?" Stad opened the folder and began flipping through the pages of lengthy blocks of text.

"Besides everyone?" Max smirked.

"Very funny."

"Specifically, the home entertainment industry. These two have apparently always been in battles, which I can believe. The movie industry has stepped it up a notch lately with some advanced tech and luxury theaters. The option to go to a movie is becoming a popular choice again with so much variety. People just aren't buying home technology as expected and seen in previous years as evidenced by the letdown this holiday season. I guess TVs can only get so big before people decide they don't need a bigger one."

"Makes sense." Stad continued scanning the paperwork. "Isn't the new tech helping them though? Don't they have a lot of that in TVs now?"

"Yeah," Max replied, "but they're just not catching on as hoped. Like I said, holiday sales didn't meet expectations and they don't seem to think that they're going to win the technological race in the long run. This time though they've come to us with an idea. It looks like they've already done a fair amount of research on it as well."

"As long as it's not the HIV needles thing again." Stad looked up from the papers.

"Careful now, I worked with the guy who came up with that idea. Trust me, it seemed more solid on paper than it actually was."

"Sure it was." Stad dove back into the paragraph he was reading.

"It's actually a pretty big scale idea. They've carefully detailed the security protocols in the majority of theaters. As you can see, the protocols are more or less nonexistent, and that's in some of the more strict theaters. There aren't any security checks up front, no ID is required to get in, they accept cash, bags aren't checked, and the list really just goes on for a while. Security cameras exist but only sparsely and of course no cameras of any kind are actually allowed in the theaters themselves. Add that to the fact that the theaters are dark and loud and it's hard to see anything in there, and well, that's a dangerous combination."

"Are you going to say what I think you're going to say?"

"That depends." Max looked at the floor and back up to face Stad with a forced smile. "How do you feel about shooting people?"

"Are they asking me to kill moviegoers?" Stad dropped the folder back down onto the desk.

"You wouldn't have to shoot to kill, just injure a few people and get the hell out of there. I think the idea is good but its implementation would be up to you."

"I don't really know how I feel about that."

"Just think about it, how laid back is the security at a movie theater anyway? You'd be completely anonymous, excluding eyewitness who are hardly accurate anyway, especially in a dark movie theater."

"That is a good point. But the risk on this one is huge. Are they prepared to pay accordingly?"

"I haven't talked in detail with them yet but I will be sure to cover the risk and expected payout for it." Max folded his hands into one another.

"I'm going to have to look into it for a little bit." Stad hesitated. "It sounds like a good plan but until I take a closer look at it I can't know for sure."

"I'll let them know that you're the professional here and I can push that message to them all day if I have to. You just look into it and let me know. They just want something implemented before blockbuster weekend, July 4th, so that gives you almost two months. And if you come across a better idea I can send it to them if it's feasible and cost-effective."

"I can do that." Stad wasn't sure there would be anything as cost-effective as hiring a lone gunman.

"Just don't rush it, this is a pretty big job."

"I can see that."

39

Stad left the office and headed for the department store tucked away in the downtown streets. It was on the corner of a busy intersection but the boring brick faded in with the rest of the background and people only knew it was there if they had been inside before. There was only a modest sign above the one entrance, but once inside it was large and expansive for anything that existed downtown. The ceilings rose high into the air and the other side could just be seen if someone looked hard enough.

The only people in the store were elderly couples with too much time on their hands. He passed them and got more than a couple of inquisitive looks with his hand over his mouth to protect him from their powerful perfumes and colognes.

His mind was swirling about the new job proposal but he tried to focus and keep his eyes at the automotive sign hovering in the background. No matter how many different ideas he tried to come up with, the one that the home entertainment industry proposed was by far the best. It bothered him, not so much the actions required for the job, but the fact that their idea was so much better than anything he could come up with. The actions were troublesome, no doubt, but he was used to injuring people and in his downtime he hunted out ways to make that happen, which was why he was standing in the middle of the automotive section of a department store in the middle of the day.

He walked down the first aisle in the section and found nothing but seat covers, window decals, rear-view mirror dice, floor mats and anything else a person would need to personalize their car. He spun around, hoping to find his target on the opposite side and his eyes searched past several different oils and fluids until he came to the end where he laid his eyes on what he wanted.

The upcoming new season meant new products on the shelves, and that often turned itself into new opportunities for Stad. The latest additions to the aisle were windshield covers, on display for the anticipated sunny summer. He grabbed one box first and flipped it over to reveal the warning label on the back. The wording on it was perfect. In the lower left corner were the words "WARNING: DO NOT DRIVE WITH WINDSHIELD COVER IN PLACE."

Stad reached for his black marker, pulled off the cap and colored in the label, leaving nothing behind but a big black box. The store hadn't anticipated a heavy demand, so after two more boxes he had to cap his marker again. He took a step back and exhaled. It was another job well done, but with an even bigger job looming over his head, he knew he had a lot more work to do.

40

Stad's life had become consumed by the movie industry job. He hadn't seen Jones, he didn't talk to Max and he ignored calls from Nikki over and over. She was persistent but he was too focused and glued to the job to pick up. It intrigued him far more than it should have. He had spent too much time trying to find alternative methods and he had finally come to the realization that he couldn't come up with a better method than the one already on the table. Over weeks he scrapped ten different ideas and felt sick to his stomach every time he had to start over. He was running out of time. He couldn't go on like this. He let go of his latest idea and turned his focus to the one presented by the clients.

He had heard of most of the movie theaters around town other than a few independent places and he pushed those to the side to focus on the larger chains. He narrowed the list to two theaters that included the giant Cineplex and the one that he and Nikki had gone to, the Sycamore 6. The Cineplex had a restaurant inside, oversized luxury seats, a daycare, the latest generation of technology and sound systems, jumbo screens, seats that were heated and rumbled and chilled cup holders. He took his time analyzing both theaters, but he decided the crowd at the Cineplex would be too large and it would be too much of a risk, so he settled on the Sycamore 6. It was an older and smaller theater but still got plenty of business from people on that side of the town. From all of his own past experiences of being a patron he knew it was employed by careless, minimum-wage teenagers who would often butter the popcorn if you asked for it or not. It was his best chance for success so he had to take it.

Currently listed as playing was a comedy that looked funny in the trailers, another comedy with an up-and-comer actress, a gory horror film, a "Best Picture" shoe in, a version of the latest comic book hero and a high adrenaline film with guns, guts, sex and the attention of every warm-blooded male. He confirmed the last movie on the list would still be showing the first week in July and he grabbed his keys.

***

A couple of car rides and large sodas later Stad was back at his apartment jotting down specifics. He captured a few notes in the theater by using his cellphone, but since it was a poor way to capture anything too detailed he had to hurry and get everything down before he could forget it all. He dug up the blueprints of the complex and the surrounding mall to help him keep it fresh in his mind and he pinned both up to his wall.

Sycamore 6 was an island of a building all its own but if it was placed just ten feet over it would be considered part of the nearby mall. The only thing getting in the way of that idea turning into reality was a small alley full of dumpsters. A large neon sign hung on the front of the building and displayed "Sycamore 6" in bright yellow and blue. Posters for the current releases hung from the brick walls that flanked the giant glass doors that made up the entrance. The ticket booth was the first thing to be seen after entering and it was staffed with unenthusiastic teenagers 90 percent of the time. The ticket booth was a small island straddled by rivers of linoleum that ran behind it and to the concession stand.

To the left of the concession stand were three theaters, the same as on the right side. "Destined for Death" was playing at the theater furthest from the entrance on the left side. At the end of both halls were fire exits, one which ran into the alleyway of dumpsters and the other into a side parking lot. There was also one fire exit per theater which ran directly to the back of the building. The entire complex, not including the mall, had exactly three security cameras. One camera was focused on the front doors, one on the ticket booth and the last was scanning the back parking lot and fire exits.

Stad decided the best time to get to work would be right before the big shootout scene when the main character delivers his line of "I see him! He's right there!" That moment occurred one hour and ten seconds into the film, not including the fifteen minutes and forty seconds of previews. Accounting for trailers, Stad calculated the moment would take place one hour, fifteen minutes and fifty seconds after the film started. He searched for a digital copy of the movie and stored it for quick reference and cross checking.

He stood up and stared at the blueprints hanging from his wall. He eyed them and tried to find something he might have missed. No matter how many times he went over something he always felt like it wasn't enough.

41

Stad sipped his coffee in a squishy booth against the back wall of a local coffee shop. Nikki had sent him a message and since he had accomplished a little bit and wanted to get out of his apartment away from tedious research, he replied. He agreed to meet her and was now waiting with his second cup of black coffee.

"And you thought I was the one who was always late." He saw her come in from the far door and greeted her as she got closer.

"Sorry." She took off her jacket and threw it into the corner of the booth. "The showing I had down here took a lot longer than I expected."

"Is it normal to have a lot of showings this far away from where you live?"

"I'm new to this team so I'm not really sure. I don't mind though." She took a deep breath. "Anything I can do to get that promotion I've been eyeing."

"I guess. You going to get anything?"

"That's why I picked this place. I'll be right back." She returned a few minutes later with a to-go cup.

"What'd you get?"

"Americano, my favorite." She took a quick sip.

"Sounds like you've been busy lately, what with all your showings," Stad said from across the booth.

"Me? You're the one who's been holed up somewhere for weeks. I haven't seen you at all."

"Is that a problem?"

"Yeah, just a little."

"It's never been one before."

"Well Stad, I can't do this forever. This relationship has to be going somewhere or I'm not sure I'm interested."

"Well what do you want from me?" Stad stared back at Nikki.

"I just want to know if you're committed at all. When I can't even reach you or talk to you I don't know what you're feeling or thinking. Do you know how many times I tried to get ahold of you the past few weeks?"

"Seven." Stad's cold voice could have chilled his drink. "And I've told you before, I'm busy, sometimes I can't answer. When you called most of the time I was either on a plane or in a meeting." Stad thought back to his phone ringing on his desk. He hated to get interrupted in the middle of research, so he hit the quiet button and kept working.

"Then what about the messages? You can't call me when you have a free minute?"

"I'm just on my own timetable, all right? It's not that I didn't want to see you, it's just that I had some other things going on and I thought you'd understand."

"How much longer are you going to be on this job?"

"I don't know, okay? Like I've said before it's not up to me. I have very little control, I just do what I'm told and that's how it is."

"Is that what this is really about?" she asked.

"What do you mean? You called me tonight."

"No." She made a pointing gesture with her hand and waved it back and forth between the two of them. "This. I really think we have something here. I'm not exactly sure what it is but I feel something and I'm not sure if you feel the same way. You just don't seem to care sometimes. I mean, we go out, have a great time together and then I don't hear from you for the longest time. What am I supposed to think?"

Stad didn't know how to respond. Most of the time the women in his life were in and out in a matter of a few hours, but Nikki was a brand new experience to him, yet somehow he was expecting this. There was a reason he kicked women out of his place so fast in the morning, it was because they wanted answers, and Stad never had any.

"I don't know what to tell you." It was all he could think of in the brief moment that he knew he had to respond. He had bought himself a couple of seconds, maybe a minute or two but eventually Nikki needed answers too. His relationship with her was different, but he didn't know what that meant. He enjoyed spending time with her but didn't want to give up his own. He found her funny, intelligent and sexy, a dangerous combination that he rarely saw. When they first started hanging out he told himself he wasn't going to get wrapped up in anything, he was living his own life and doing his own thing and he didn't want that to stop. Then he realized how much fun he had with her and maybe the other stuff didn't matter as much, but he still couldn't bring himself around to the idea.

"I mean," Stad continued and watched Nikki fidget with her lid, "I think we do have something but I just don't know where to take it from here. I think you're great and sexy and the time we spend together is great, but-"

"But what?" Nikki jumped at the chance to say anything.

"But I don't know. I'm sorry, I don't know." Stad expected an angry backlash, screaming and flailing, but instead just saw Nikki stop messing with her cup lid and sip her drink. Just when he was expecting an outburst, Stad got calmness and he remembered what was so different about her.

"Well I'll tell you what Stad, in a couple of weeks the zoo is having their season opening and I thought it'd be fun to go. Who knows, maybe they'll have some mutant hybrid animals this year." She looked up from her mug and smiled. "If you feel like it you can meet me there when it opens. If I don't see you, I'll know it just wasn't the right timing for us to try to start something. How's that sound?"

"I think that's a good idea."

"I just don't want you to do anything you don't want to do."

Stad didn't have to answer.

"I'm sorry I dragged you all the way here for this, but I just felt it was something I had to tell you in person." Nikki picked up her jacket and stood up.

"I'm glad you did, I think," Stad said.

"If I don't see you, have a good life." She turned and headed for the door. The bell attached above clinked and Stad watched her walk out and down the sidewalk. He sat in the far back table until his coffee was gone.

42

In the middle of recalculating the timing of his job, Stad got a phone call. Before answering, he tilted his head back and looked away at the ceiling giving his eyes a much-needed rest from the screen.

"Yeah?"

"It's Max."

"What's up?"

"You've got the go-ahead on the water job. I just spoke with them and they think that now is the right time to set the pieces in motion. Can you get your guy on it soon?"

"He's been expecting a call from me for a while now, I'll let him know." Stad shuffled some papers around and looked for an empty spot on any of them where he could write down a note to himself. "Did they provide any more details about numbers or distribution?"

"Nothing. They didn't seem to care too much about numbers but liked the idea and told us to move forward. I was expecting a little more too, sorry."

"That's all right." Stad dropped his pen and leaned back in his chair. "I'll give my supplier a call and let him know what's going on and when he has more information I'll bring you back into the loop."

"As long as it gets done fast. I don't want them to be waiting on us, that's bad for business."

"Yeah well, with the amount of time we waited for a response are they really in a position to be pushy?"

"They're paying the bills, of course they are."

"Yeah." Stad wasn't sure why he made that comment. "It won't be a problem."

"What about the movie job, what's the word on that?" Max jumped into the next topic.

"It's solid. I mean their plan that is. I couldn't come up with anything better. It's looking like we'll be a go at this point but I just have a few more things to wrap up before I can provide an official report." Stad always put off writing the report until the end since it was busywork that he hated.

"I'm not sure they're looking for a detailed report, it was indicated to me that they've done a lot of the research themselves."

"So you're saying I don't need to put one together?" Stad held his breath. He hadn't been able to get by without a report since working against the airlines a few years back.

"I'd hold off on that until I know for sure. I'm supposed to hear from them again soon and I'll let you know after that. They'll be eager to hear any new details then if you have any."

"Yeah." Stad glanced at his papers and pulled up some documents on his screen. "The first weekend of July is going to work well. I'm going to shoot for Saturday night, which seems to give me the best options."

"Good one." Max laughed.

"What?"

"You're going to *shoot* for Saturday?"

"Very funny Max, this is serious."

"Sorry."

"Saturday looks like the best bet, early evening, so if they want an update they should expect one around that time. It's a local theater, Sycamore 6 and 'Destined for Death' is the target movie, it's really loud and obnoxious so it'll be perfect."

"That'll probably be enough to tide them over for now. I think they really just wanted to know where we sat on the timeline."

"We'll meet theirs, no problem," Stad said.

"I wouldn't expect anything else from you. I'll give them that but I need to let you go so you can put the other job in motion. Let me know the details on that when they're in, otherwise I'll call you."

"Sounds good, talk to you later." Stad ended the call and before forgetting any of the details he dialed his supplier. In typical fashion, the phone rang for almost a full two minutes before there was any answer.

"Yeah?" The supplier's voice was as raspy as it always had been.

"It's Stad. We've got a go-ahead on the water job."

"Perfect." There was a crackle in the background. "The inside man has been on the job for a while just waiting, so he should be ready to go when I give him a call. Do they want this done right away?"

"Yep, as soon as you can."

"How about right after we hang up."

"That's perfect, keep me filled in, all right?"

"In all of the years we've worked together have I ever not filled you in?"

"No, just giving a friendly reminder." Stad backtracked. "That's why I always come back to you. Speaking of, a new job just came in. It's a high visibility, high priority project."

"Fresh meat, I like it. What do you need?"

"Not sure 100 percent on everything but I know I'll need at least one thing. What kind of guns can you get ahold of?"

"Now we're talking. I can get you anything you need but you're going to have to be more specific."

"Well the plan isn't complete yet, but I know I'll need something small and muffled. I'll be in a smaller room with maybe 30 to 50 people inside. It's a loud place with lots of commotion, but I don't want anyone outside the room to notice too much."

"What's the job?"

"It's against the movie industry. I'll be open firing in a movie theater."

"Damn."

"You okay with that?" Stad ran his hand through his hair.

"Yeah, yeah, I can get you the right tool for the job. You'll need a silencer but I should let you know it's not like in the movies. It's still going to make some noise, just make sure you have a good escape route planned."

"Believe me," Stad said, "there's plenty of planning that still needs to go into this one."

"Well whoever's after these guys, I hope it's worth it for them."

"Since the risk is so high our payouts are going to increase. I don't know exact numbers yet, but if it gives you some extra motivation, feel free to use it."

"I'll keep that in mind, but it makes no difference in the quality of my work."

"Good to know."

"Where do you want me to send it?"

The problem that Stad encountered the most was actually getting his supplies without suspicion. On a few occasions he had to drive to meet up with his supplier and take the equipment back himself, other times he was able to have it shipped to an agreed upon location and in the rarest of circumstances he could fly down there and bring it back on the plane, but ever since regulations were locked up it had been harder to do that. Stad hated driving down there to get his stuff and that was always his last resort, it was much more convenient for both parties to have it shipped somewhere.

"Still got the details on the storage unit for the bombs? You can send it there."

"You got it. When do you need it by?"

"At the very latest, fourth of July weekend, but I'd like to have it in as soon as you can get ahold of it."

"I'll work on it."

"Make sure it's untraceable."

"Didn't we just talk about this?" his supplier asked. "You should know me better than that. When has anything I've ever given you been able to be traced anywhere?"

"I know, just checking."

"All right, is that all? I'd like to get moving on this water job." There was a thumping sound in the background, like one of a hand slapping against a crate.

"All for now. Talk to you shortly."

"You got it." The line went dead and Stad went back to his research.

43

"Long time no see, how's the girl treating you?" Jones passed a glass full of scotch and seven to Stad, slumped at his usual stool.

"I didn't tell you? I thought I told you about all of that."

"Not me, you haven't been in here in weeks."

"Yeah I've been chained to my desk."

"Well what's going on?" Jones stopped looking around for other customers and leaned against the bar.

"She basically gave me a choice. I either choose her or I choose myself." Stad picked up his drink and downed a fourth of it.

"What's that supposed to mean?"

"She seems to think we don't see eye to eye on our relationship, which is actually true. She wants to know if I'm dedicated to it or not."

"Well that's a simple answer. Are you?"

"That's just the thing. I have no idea. I mean, one day it's just me and I'm in here and across the street and having fun, then the next day I'm out with her and having fun with her. I just don't know what happened."

"Women can be tricky like that."

"It's not that she tricked me or anything, I would rather be with her than any other woman around."

"Yep. That's what happens."

"I've been thinking about it a lot though, ever since she talked to me about it. I just can't seem to shake the fact that it just feels right, you know? I mean, the more I try to reason with myself into thinking I shouldn't be with her, the more I just strengthen the other side of the argument." Stad took another fourth out of his glass.

"Stad, over the years I've heard lots of stories from lots of different people. Some are uplifting, some are depressing, some are great and others are boring. You know what I see in yours? I've heard everything from you, everything except having something with meaning. It sounds like your job means a lot to you, and there's nothing wrong with that, but I've never heard you talk about anything else. No hobbies, no family, no meaningful relationships, no women, not counting those bimbos you take back to your place. I've never heard anything with more substance, you know?"

"Yeah." Stad set his drink back down.

"And I've heard it before, so you're not alone, but in the end I think it's just the next step, a natural progression. I don't think it's a bad thing like you think it is, in fact I think it'd be worse if you never experienced it."

"I don't know Jones, I mean, I feel like my whole life is changing."

"You do know Stad, I can tell."

Stad knew what he was hearing from Jones was right. The reason he enjoyed being with Nikki was because it was something he had been missing and always wanted but never knew it. Jones explained it so simply and shed some light on it for him. He took another drink, set the glass back on the table and stared into the murky liquid. It was worth the risk. Something had to change, he didn't want to end up an old man throwing back drinks in the same spot and trying to pick up women half his age. He couldn't picture himself down the road chatting with an even older Jones about a fake job and pretending to have emotions.

"I think you're right," Stad said after a long silence.

"I know. I get that a lot." A smile appeared on the old man's face.

"I can't believe I've been so stupid."

"Believe me," Jones said, "I've seen stupid people, and you're definitely not one of them. Sometimes you just need someone to talk to and it all gets sorted out."

"You've helped a bunch, Jones. Thanks." Stad had always felt his life was one giant cliché, coming into the same bar every night and talking to the same bartender, but now that he had received helpful advice on one of his life's problems, he knew that cliché had been solidified.

"It's a good thing I charge two hundred dollars an hour."

"Put it on my tab." Stad smiled and finished off his half-full drink.

44

Suit #1 was not present but his female assistant had joined the rest of the suits for the latest update on their dilemma. She sat in her same chair near the head of the table, next to the man in the black suit who was sitting in #1's chair and trying to fill the big void as best as possible, minus the cigarette smoke. He was still wearing his blackest suit and adjusted his black tie before he began.

"Good news." He grasped the table and tried to be as intimidating as possible. "We have set up plans with the company and their contact has assured us they have the proper resources and abilities to pull it off. He gave us the exact date, location and rough time that it's going to take place, so we will reconvene at that moment and hold an all hands meeting. It's the first weekend in July, just in time to strike during the summer blockbusters." He paused to take a swig from his glass of water. The room was mulling over the fact that their plan was now turning into reality. "This meeting is absolutely, 100 percent required. We're in this together and if anything happens I need everyone here, all day if we have to. We need contingency plans, damage control plans if necessary, the PR team and the entire brigade on deck." He looked around the room and saw the other suits sweating in their chairs. "We can't go back now, so let's hope for the best."

The assistant seated next to him scratched down notes as fast as her hand could keep up while the rest of the room was motionless and still pondering the words they had just heard. A few of the men scratched their faces, others looked down at the floor, some rocked backward in their chairs and the Three Bald Mice looked back at the man in black with nothing but discontent splattered across their faces. They still resented every minute they were in the room with him.

"So what's the plan now?" one of the suits asked.

"We wait. We wait to see what happens. We'll meet here that Saturday and go forward. When news comes in of the outcome we'll make our decisions based on whatever we know at that time. Unfortunately until that moment arrives, there's nothing we can do but wait."

45

The zoo opened at nine in the morning, which was early for Stad, but he was in the parking lot at 8:45. Dozens of thoughts ran through his head and half of them were about Nikki. He chomped on the piece of spearmint gum in his mouth and wondered if he was making the right decision. At five to the hour he stepped out of his car and purchased two admittance tickets. He found a nice spot in the shade of a tall oak tree and waited. His thoughts started running faster and faster and became overwhelming until he was put out of his misery. His thoughts faded away and his mind became a blank slate when he saw a beautiful figure emerge from the horizon. He knew right away that it was her from the way her hair blew in the slight breeze to the way her hips wiggled with each step. When she got closer the breeze picked up and sent a strawberry aroma his way. When she stepped out of the shadows and into the sun her smiling face was reflected back at his. She walked closer and lifted her hands up and out and when she was close to Stad he took a step forward and they embraced.

"I knew you'd be here." Nikki pulled away but stayed close.

"I just had some thinking to do, but I always knew in my gut that I'd be here too."

"So this means you're okay with everything?"

"I've had a lot of time to think about it," Stad said, "and I am more than okay with everything. I'm just glad you brought it to my attention, because I don't think I could have gotten over that hump without you."

"I'm just trying to help." Nikki smiled.

"Want to see if they have any of those infamous hybrid animals?" Stad reached into his pocket, pulled out the two tickets and held them out between his fingers.

"I wouldn't want to be doing anything else."

They got around half of the park before stopping for lunch at a small food stand. They didn't get around the other half but finished up their day by watching the polar bears splash around in the water and the penguins slide on the ice. It was still early when they left the park and Stad had other plans.

"Can I show you something?" Stad stopped in the middle of the parking lot. "It's something I've been meaning to show you and I told you I would when the time was right, and I think that time is now."

"Are you going to show me your weird hobby?" Nikki perked up.

"It's not weird, it's different. Collecting leaves is weird, this is not that."

"I'll be the judge of that."

"All right." Stad started walking again. "Are you okay with leaving your car here?"

"Sure, we can pick it up later. I don't think they close until later tonight anyway." Nikki kept pace with Stad. "So are you going to tell me or just let it be a total surprise?"

"Where's the fun in telling you?" They laughed and walked the rest of the way to the car. Stad pulled out of the lot and got onto the highway.

"Where are we going?" Nikki asked from the passenger seat.

"I told you, it's a surprise." Stad turned to look at Nikki staring out the window. He could see the reflection of her wrinkled forehead in the glass. "Don't worry. You trust me, right?"

"Of course," she said, still staring off in the distance. After a few more miles Stad took the left exit onto a main road and then took another left to climb up a hill. When they got to the top he could see a familiar glow of fluorescent lights.

"We're not going there are we?"

"You'll see." Stad steered the car down the hill and toward the enormous Supercenter parking lot.

"I'm starting to get a little creeped out again, Stad. What is it exactly that you do?"

"I'm just trying to put some common sense back into the world." He parked and tried to hustle around the front end to open Nikki's door but she had already beaten him to it.

"Still not sure where you're going with this."

"You'll understand once you see." Stad locked the doors.

"It's not one of those Robin Hood things where you steal for a supposed good cause, is it? I don't feel like getting hauled off to jail tonight."

"No, it's not. As far as I know it's perfectly legal." Stad shrugged. "I mean, I've never been arrested for doing it."

"When you start a sentence with 'As far as I know' in relation to the legality of something, it's usually not a good sign."

"I guess some people might consider it a gray area, but aren't they all?" They walked past minivans, SUVs and stray shopping carts on their way to the entrance. The front doors opened and they were greeted with even more fluorescent lights and endless rows of shelves with crap piled on them.

"I don't know what it is about this place but it gives me the creeps," Nikki said as they passed a train of shopping carts.

"Creepier than all those exhibits at the museum?" Stad scanned the giant signs that hung over each row.

"It's close."

"I get that feeling too." Stad's head swiveled from right to left and Nikki noticed.

"What are you looking for?" she asked.

"I'm not exactly sure where they are but I'm looking for wherever the power tools are." Stad strode across the floor and tried to avoid the crowds of people shopping for deals on everything from flatware to tennis shoes and even an entire section for July 4th decorations.

"Remember when I asked you if you were going to bury me under your apartment?" Nikki asked, following Stad down the walkway. He didn't return a response. "Well now that you're telling me we're looking for power tools, those thoughts are starting to float back into my head."

"Relax, you're in a public space now with lots of bright lights, you'll be fine." Stad dodged a few more center kiosks and oversized people and kept his eyes toward the banners.

"Are they going to be in with the 'Home Maintenance' section?" Nikki pointed to the opposite corner of the store. Stad turned around and followed her finger to the area.

"Perfect." Stad started walking in the opposite direction and dodged customers scrambling for the last day deals on new plastic containers.

"Can I help you?" A young man stepped in their way. His nametag said "Scott" and his face said 17.

"Nope," Stad said mid stride and kept going past the teenager. Nikki stopped to say thanks before catching up to Stad.

"You don't have to be so rude."

"Neither does he."

"He was just trying to help," Nikki insisted.

"I wasn't aware that I looked like I needed any help."

"Well you couldn't find the section you were looking for."

"You're right, sorry." Stad sighed and turned to face her. "Now if you want to use those sharp eyes of yours and help me find the drills that would be great."

"You mean those drills?" She nodded at the display set up just beyond the table saws.

"I'm glad I brought you along this time." Stad stepped over and stopped in front of the shelf full of drills. He grabbed one and looked over it in his hands for half a minute while Nikki stood in silence.

"Found what I was looking for." He handed the box to Nikki and pointed the warning label out to her.

"Warning," Nikki read out loud, "this product not intended for use as a dental drill." She looked up at Stad with a glazed look.

"Why is that on the box?" he asked, hoping to shed some light on the issue.

"I guess the company has to cover its ass."

"Then why isn't there a warning telling me not to turn it on and stick it in my foot? This warning is only here because someone tried to do exactly what it's saying not to."

"I suppose," she said. "But everything's got some kind of warning, I don't see what the big deal is."

"The big deal," Stad said as he grabbed the box out of her hands, "is that we're warning people about things that should be common sense and it's making everyone just a little dumber." He pulled his black marker out of his back pocket.

"What's that for?" Nikki asked.

"I'm going to cover up this label as best I can to make it seem like it never existed." He pulled off the cap and started tracing over the label.

"Wait." Nikki shouted in the middle of the store. She caught herself and looked around, hoping Scott or any other employees hadn't heard. She lowered her voice. "You can't do that."

"Why not?" Stad stopped tracing and held the box in one hand. "It's just a stupid label."

"Because that's just not right. What if it causes someone to get seriously injured, or worse, what if they end up dying?"

"Let's be honest, if that was the reason somebody died, wouldn't the world be better off without them?"

Nikki stepped forward and hit Stad in the shoulder hard enough to send him a message. "That's terrible. Just because someone's not as smart as you or needs different messages than you doesn't mean that they're just a waste of space. You can't just assume, Stad."

"Well-"

"No, I don't want to hear it. You have no right to tell people what common sense is and you especially have no right to decide who lives and who dies."

"That's ridiculous, I'm not playing some kind of god here, Nikki."

"You're certainly influencing it, aren't you?"

"Only by a very small margin." Stad looked back at her.

"I can't believe you'd be so careless with the potential to destroy a human life. You've obviously considered the impact before and yet you still go through with it? What if someone else found a message stupid and obvious that you thought was really helpful and they removed it?"

"I wouldn't need a common sense label though. These are just so painfully obvious that they shouldn't even exist."

"There's no such thing as common sense, Stad. What's common to some might not be to others. This is a dangerous game you're playing."

"People should still know better."

"Even if that's true there are much better ways to go about getting your message across, don't you think?" Nikki rested her hands on her hips.

"There may be more productive ways, sure, but this is the easiest and you have to admit, it's effective."

"I don't know Stad, I just don't like it. I really wish you would stop. How long have you been doing this anyway?"

"A few years at least, I'm not really sure when I started." Stad stared at the half-covered warning label on the box in his hand. "I guess I can give it a rest for now." He placed the box back on the shelf. "I just wanted to be open with you and show you something more personal."

"No, I really appreciate it, and I'm glad you're okay with opening up to me a little more."

"Well it's the least I could do after everything you've done for me."

"I haven't done anything for you Stad, you've done it yourself." Nikki stepped in again and kissed him. "But seriously, you carry a black marker around with you all the time?"

"Not all the time. I carry markers of all colors in my car, and a bottle of whiteout just in case. I know it's weird, but-"

"I told you it was weird," Nikki interrupted. "But I can understand. If I see a neat leaf I'll pick it up and carry it around with me until I get home. Everyone has something weird. Maybe some other time I'll show you my collection."

"I'd like to see that." Stad smiled, grabbed her hand and headed for the exit.

"Are you busy later in the week? Maybe you can come over to my place. I'll even make you dinner if you want."

"You know you don't have to do that, right?" Stad couldn't remember the last time somebody cooked a meal for him.

"I know, but I'm going to anyway." She smiled.

"Thanks." Stad couldn't think of much else to say.

"How's Friday at six?" Nikki asked.

"That should be fine."

"You don't have any food allergies or anything, do you?"

"I'm not allergic but I hate pepperoni."

"I don't think I have any recipes that call for pepperoni, but if I do I'll make sure I throw them out." They got closer to the car before Nikki said anything again. "This is going to be fun," she blurted in the middle of the parking lot.

"Yeah," Stad replied. He wanted to think about it, but the only thing running through his head was his busy week. He struggled with his thoughts the entire time he was driving back to the zoo to get Nikki's car.

46

Stad tried to get some work done, but every time he tried
to clear his mind it would just end up being occupied with
thoughts of Nikki. He never imagined an outing to Supercenter
would change the way he thought, but now that he had time to
think over Nikki's words, they hit him with more meaning each
time.

Why was he harming these innocent people?

Her view changed his outlook and now he was struggling
to rationalize walking into a movie theater with a loaded gun.
Every time it ran through his head the only thing he could hear
was her voice and the only thing he could see was her face. She
was everyone in the theater. She was the tall man in the front
who should have sat closer to the back, she was the couple in the
last row that never made a sound, she was the family in the
middle straggling behind and walking in midway through the
previews, she was the group of teenagers who checked their
phones every two minutes. He was the lone one out, sitting in a
crowd of familiar faces but feeling uncomfortable and out of
control.

He got up and walked over to the bathroom to splash his
face with cold water and tried to refocus. He sat back down and
went over details like where he'd put his gun, which seat he
would take and how much time he'd be in the theater before
making his exit. He was able to block out some of his thoughts

and continued planning things like where he'd park his car, how he'd ditch it afterwards and where he'd change clothes. When the thoughts of Nikki's words came flooding back he forced them aside and hoped that once he got inside the theater he would be able to do the same.

He was distracted for a while by a phone call from his supplier. The man on the inside at the water company had been able to contaminate the water supply without any trouble and the tainted product was being shipped at the end of the day.

Finally, some good news.

He wanted to keep Max up-to-date but knew that he'd have to do it in person. He looked at the clock and decided he had time to get in his practice run first.

He focused on the tasks of driving on his way. Stop sign here, pedestrian there, yield to this car, that guy has the right of way, why are you hurting innocent people? He parked his car off in the side lot with nine other vehicles. It was a safer bet than parking in the back all by himself and drawing the attention of the manager on his smoke break.

Stad stepped up to the box office and handed over his cash for the matinee. As expected, the show was still playing at the last theater down the far left hallway. He made a stop at the concession stand first.

"What would you like?" It was another minimum-wage teenager behind a counter.

"Just a couple of candy bars."

"What kind?"

What kind? He hadn't thought about that. All the little things that tripped other people up were starting to get to Stad. He had spent too much time worrying about Nikki and the thoughts she had put into his head instead of the details. He panicked, had all this hard work been exposed by a high school junior? Stay calm, he thought. Nothing's suspicious. Not yet.

"Just two plain chocolate bars, whatever you have."

"Let me check, just a second."

Stad didn't want to be here. He wanted to be with Nikki. She was the only one who really understood him and could help him now. He watched the teenager dig around the candy in the back and wondered if he'd be impacted at all. What if he lost his job? What if his friends were at the movie at the same time? He's just trying to make a living, probably saving for a new car or something. He came back up to the counter carrying two large candy bars.

"Are these okay? They're the only plain ones we have, everything else has caramel or nuts or something."

"Yeah, that's fine." It didn't matter, they were just going to be used in place of a gun and silencer.

"It's going to be eight dollars."

"Here you go." Stad paid in cash. "Thanks." He took the candy and made another quick stop in the bathroom. He found an empty stall and tucked one of the chocolate bars into his pants and the other on the opposite side. He tried to imagine they were both several times heavier. He stepped out and walked over to the sink. He looked miserable. The face in the mirror didn't seem like his anymore. It was more worn down than he had ever seen. He splashed his face and dried off with the cheap paper towels. He walked out to the last theater on the left and tried to focus on how the candy bars moved with every step.

The door for "Destined for Death" was the last one before the fire exit leading out to the alleyway. Once inside there were two paths that both curled around to the stadium seats. Like any other movie theater the halls and stairs were lined with little lights. Stad followed the lights up to the first landing and then to the third row from the back of the room, below the projection room. He knew that people were always suspicious of those in the back row, so he avoided it. His seat was closest to the aisle as well in case a quick exit was needed.

Stad sat down in the extra plush chair and the candy bars squished between his legs and the arm rests. He looked around and found the two front exits on either side of the screen, knowing he'd have to keep good watch on them for anyone trying to escape. He'd also have to do the same for the side exits leading to the main door. His vantage point to the exit on the side furthest from him was good enough to where he could spot people trying to leave, but for the exit on his side, his sight was restricted by a half wall and railing. He stood up and went over to the half wall and did some convincing stretches while eyeing the exit. By standing up just a little he had a much better view of the closer exit and if he walked over to it he could cover it without compromising his view across the theater. Stad sat back down and worked out how he thought people would react. The people closest to him would be the most dangerous threat to the plan and they would either try to fight back, stand up and start running or be in such a state of shock that they'd just sit there, staring at the mysterious gunman and unable to move.

Stad imagined slowing the crowd down while at the same time eyeing the exits. The movie would be loud enough where some people would not notice until it was too late. He'd be the center of the ripple effect sent throughout the crowd. He pictured himself moving down each step, scanning the people for any signs of retaliation, escape or the unexpected. With each imagined step his head was on a swivel. More people started to notice him but his focus moved from those in the back and around him to those just starting to realize what was happening. Most of them were sitting while a few others tried to take cover on the sticky floor. He reached the first landing and focused on those toward the front who were hearing things now and moving around in their seats. Even more people jumped on the floor and crouched behind their seats and pretended like their popcorn was bulletproof.

He reached the main floor and strafed toward the front. Everyone was now aware of what was going on but nobody could move. The few that had tried had failed and were lying slumped against their own body weight on the floor. The noise and commotion picked up but blended in with the soundtrack of the movie and the cries on screen couldn't be distinguished between those coming from the front rows.

Stad reached the exit door and made one last scan around for stragglers or last minute heroes and when nobody presented themselves as a threat he kicked backward and knocked open the exit door. Once outside he turned around, tucked his guns away and slammed the door shut.

Stad's mind was drawn back into the present and he became aware of the theater now partly filled with people waiting for the matinee to begin. The lights dimmed and the screen flickered to life. Stad ran his hand over his face as the previews began rolling.

***

"I see him! He's right there!" The cue blared through the surround sound and wanting to make it as close to the real thing as possible, Stad got up from his seat and took the steps one at a time. Explosions and gunfire flashed back and forth on the screen, but he didn't care to watch it again. The scenario played out in his mind again only with a detour to the side exit instead of the one near the front. If he took the exit near the screen people would be too suspicious. He tried to keep the images in his head of what he had previously seen.

When he reached the main hallway he left through the double doors at the end that led out to the alley. He walked past the dumpsters and found the back exit of the theater he was just in. He got up close to the door and pretended like he had just slammed it shut and holstered his gun.

He knew that a horror movie had just ended and people would be leaving. He hadn't expected many to be in attendance of a gory film in the middle of the day but a few of them began to pour out the back exit. He picked up his pace and followed them out to the front parking lot, hoping there'd be a lot more moviegoers on a Saturday night. He blended in with the crowd all the way to his car, where he hopped in and threw his almost liquefied chocolate bars in the glove compartment. He was successful in blocking out Nikki's words for a while but they began to start pouring back in. He started to drive away and got the feeling that when it was time to do the job, it wouldn't be even half as easy as it was today.

47

On his way to see Max, Stad made a pit stop at a kitchen boutique stored wedged into an older building downtown. The only indication that the store existed was an oversize stainless steel knife affixed to the wall with bold letters that spelled out "Kitchen Etc." Stad parked in a tiny parking lot across the street. Once inside the store, it opened up and reached into every available crevice. It no longer felt like a boutique store downtown but a corner store in a mega mall. From the ceiling on down there were stacks of kitchen gadgets, flatware and expensive looking China.

"Can I help you?" A lady in a bright red apron popped her head out from behind a tower of small electronic appliances. Her hair and makeup were perfected and she was dressed straight out of a housekeeping magazine. She looked like the type of person that spent the holidays getting every dab of frosting perfect on heaps of homemade cookies.

"I'm just looking, thanks." Stad hurried on and tried to round the corner.

"Just to let you know, we're having a special on knives this week and if you buy one set, you get a set of three cutting boards for free."

"Knives?" Stad paused and turned to face the homemaker. "I could use some new ones, where are they?"

"Let me show you." The lady started walking down a narrow, defined walkway.

"You can just point them out." Stad stopped her. "I was going to wander around anyway to see if I needed something else."

"Sure." She stood on the tips of her toes and pointed above and beyond another small stack of boxes. "They're in that corner and the sale ends tomorrow. My name's Nancy if you need help or have any questions."

"Thanks." Stad headed in the direction Nancy had started down only a few moments ago. She seemed to be the only staff member in the store and was out of Stad's sightline in a couple of short steps.

Thoughts about the job started creeping back into his brain and he and felt that he was in a no-win situation. Nikki's words had resonated with him more than he expected. He started analyzing all the choices he was making and reflecting back on previous decisions. Never before had he had any reservations about a job, but with Nikki's input, this one had become much different. He felt that it crossed a line that he wasn't sure he was prepared to do. He wasn't even sure if he wanted to do any jobs ever again. He was in agony over just this one and couldn't imagine going forward and suffering through the same thing all over again. However, if he went through with this job then he could tell Max he was done. He could go out with a bang, on top of his game, with a large payout to the firm and the backing of his boss. But if he backed down now, not only would Max be upset, the home entertainment industry would be furious and the guillotine would start dropping. The industry couldn't face the risk of having Max and Stad running around with knowledge of what they wanted to accomplish and they would make sure that wouldn't be a problem.

The decision haunted his thoughts. With one option he would be harming the lives of people he had never met, and with the second option he'd be harming those that were closest to him. Max and his family would be ruined and Stad would never be heard from again.

What if the industry knew about Nikki?

Stad's mind flashed back to the theater. He was surrounded by people who were just looking to get away. There were couples sitting close to each other and holding hands. There were people playing jokes on one another and just laughing. There were people that reminded him of Nikki and him. If he went through with it, these people would never be the same.

Is that something I can live with?

He snapped back to the store and leaned in toward the wall of knife boxes to read the words on each. A few claimed to cut through what it said others couldn't, while some others claimed to be used by the top chefs worldwide. He laid eyes on a set in a black box and picked it up and flipped it over. As expected, on the back next to the picture of the knives displayed on a cutting board were the words "Use caution: Knives are sharp."

Instincts caused him to reach for the black marker in his back pocket but he stopped. This wasn't much different than what he was being asked to do in the movie theater. His actions here could send a ripple through someone's life, similar to how his actions on the job would send many ripples through many different lives.

If he said no he knew the witch hunt would start at the top and wouldn't stop until it hit the bottom. People in the home entertainment industry who were involved in the choice would be impacted, Max would be hurt and the final blow would be to Stad and perhaps Nikki, who he wanted to protect no matter the cost. If he said yes the most obvious people impacted would be those who chose to go to the movie at the same time as him. Not only would they be hurt emotionally and physically, their families would never be the same. Theaters nationwide would be impacted and there was no way he could predict the outcome downstream.

Stad walked back to the counter with one of the knife boxes and tried to reason himself into some middle ground. If he went through with it he would get a lot of money, which he could turn around and use for a good cause. He could donate it to a hospital to be put to better use, he could give it to a research institute and have his terrible actions be the reason that cancer was cured. There were a million things he could do with it, and although the idea seemed far-fetched it was plausible, and much better than some alternatives.

"Find everything all right?" Nancy asked as Stad approached the register.

"Actually I'm still kind of undecided, but this seems like the best bet for now." Stad put the box on the counter.

"Is it anything I can help with? Answer a few questions you have maybe?"

"No, this'll be fine for now." He got back to his car and threw the knives and cutting boards onto the passenger seat. He gripped the steering wheel until his knuckles turned white. The choice wasn't going to be an easy one and now that it was getting closer to becoming reality, it was even harder. He knew he couldn't make the decision by himself.

48

"Max, open up." Stad banged against the solid door separating Max's office from the hallway. He gave a few more thumps and then stood back and listened. After hearing nothing but silence he stepped forward and banged his fists a couple more times. "Come on." The desperation oozed out of his voice and after another minute of silence he pressed the intercom button and squeaked out "Number 92." The door clicked open and he stormed in. "Come on, what the hell? You knew it was me."

"And you know the rules." Max was standing with his hands resting on the desk. It looked like he was reviewing papers. "Did the bottled water job get kicked off all right?"

"Yeah, I let my supplier know."

"What'd he say? Does he have everything?"

"Max, I have to talk to you about the movie job." Stad paced on the other side of the desk.

"What is it?"

"That's just it, I don't know."

"What do you mean?" Max took his hands off the desk and stood at Stad's eye level.

"I'm just not sure if I can do it."

"I can't have you back out on me now, the job's this weekend, Stad."

"I know you told them I could pull it off anyway, so why are you worried?" Stad stared into Max's eyes and took his silence as affirmation. "You know that puts me in a bind, right?"

"Why? Why are you having such a hard time with this one?"

"I'm not sure, it's just different this time."

"Not really," Max said. "It's just another job. Nothing's ever taken you this long to get your shit together on. What's going on?"

"Things have changed. I've been thinking about it a lot."

"Why?"

"Does it matter?"

"Stad." Max adjusted his wristwatch. "I know you've run through all the scenarios by now and hell, have probably done a practice run already, right?"

"That's not the point."

"Well I'm sure you're aware of all the consequences of your actions, right?"

"Yeah, that's what made me stop and think about it."

"What do you mean?"

"I mean I'm having a hard time accepting the fact that if I go through with this I'm going to have to kill some random strangers."

"First off," Max replied, "nobody said you had to kill anybody, I'm not sure why that's stuck in your head. And secondly, if you do the opposite and don't go through with it, you can kiss your own ass goodbye. Probably mine too."

"I know but-"

"Let me put it more simply. If you don't do this, we're done, finished, we won't have lives anymore, they'll take it all.

We'll either be out on the streets or under the ground. Finished. You have to do this, you understand that, right?"

"I don't think it's as simple as you want it to be." Stad grabbed the back of the chair and leaned against it.

"I don't care if it is or not, it's still your job."

"So are you going to fire me if I don't do it?"

"Let's not jump ahead, all right?" Max waved his arms in the air.

"No, I'm serious. I really don't know if I want to be in this business anymore."

"What are you trying to say?

"If I go through with this…" Stad paused and tried to gauge Max's feelings. "What do you think the chances are of me getting out of here?"

"I don't know, you caught me off guard, I wasn't expecting this." Max crossed his arms. "Is it something we have to come to terms on now?"

"No, but I want a promise from you that if I do this, we'll at least talk seriously about it and you'll give me fair options."

"Yeah, sure, we can talk about it depending on how this job goes. Let's just focus on getting that done first. Does that help? Do you feel better about things?"

"Not a whole lot," Stad said.

"Well what else do you want from me?"

"I don't know."

"I can sit here and help you rationalize any decision you want me to, but I know you've already decided what you're going to do. I knew what your decision was going to be the day I told you about the job, that's why I told them we'd do it." Max fiddled with his watch again.

"I just want you to know that things are changing and that you might have to find yourself a new go-to guy."

"Honestly Stad, as long as he doesn't start doubting himself it wouldn't bother me."

"Sometimes I hate this job." Stad said it out loud but thought he hadn't.

"Don't we all?" Max replied. There was a moment of silence before Max asked about the water industry job. "So what'd your supplier say about the bottled water stuff?"

"He's got the ball rolling in the capping plant already, so we should start seeing those hit the shelves in less than a week." Stad's eyes never left the floor.

"Same targets I assume?"

"Of course."

"All right, we'll keep our eyes out on reports."

Stad sighed.

"Hey Stad." Max looked up from the papers on the desk after a while. "I know you'll make the right choice about this."

"What if the right choice isn't the one I thought it was?" Stad looked up from the ground.

"It's still the right one."

49

The job consumed Stad's thoughts. He was used to distractions but this one was larger than any other. After a trek he reached "Parkview Place" and pulled around to a visitor parking spot close to Nikki's building. He jumped out into the warm summer air and walked around the lighted pond to the elevators, waited for them to take him up to her door and waited again after knocking. He could hear her footsteps from the outside.

"Hey." Nikki swung open the door.

"You look amazing as usual." Stad took a long look at her legs in her mini skirt, matched with a kind of top that he didn't know the name of.

"Thanks, you too."

"It's pretty nice out." He removed his light jacket and tried to find a place to put it.

"You can put that in there if you want." Nikki pointed to the closet.

"Sure." He slipped his coat onto one of the two available hangers. The closet was empty except for the lone open hanger and a few of Nikki's coats. He closed the door and looked around the apartment and noticed it was in the exact same state as last time.

"Would you say you're more of a minimalist, Nikki?" Stad asked.

"Not really, why?"

"Well there isn't a whole lot to your apartment. There's an empty closet, hardly any furniture, nothing on the walls…"

"Yeah I know and it's driving me crazy. Since I'm trying to buy a house I didn't want to unpack everything and start rearranging things if I was just going to move in another month or so. I know it sounds lazy, but it's so much easier."

"You don't have to tell me that." Stad sat down on one of the stools at the counter.

"Plus between work and everything else I don't have a lot of time for it either."

"Everything else like stalking me?"

"I do have a life outside of you, you know."

"I forgot, you collect leaves too." Stad laughed.

"Very funny."

"Sorry, besides I don't think it's fair of me to judge anyone else's living space. I mean, you've seen mine, right?"

"Yeah, and it wasn't really that bad. I've seen worse." Nikki walked into the kitchen. "Oh, I almost forgot, do you want anything to drink? I have a few different wines and some beer. Sorry, I'm all out of scotch."

"That's all right, I'll just take a beer." He watched Nikki reach into the fridge and pull out a bottle. She opened it and handed it to him before going back to inspect whatever it was she was making. "What are you cooking?"

"I've got some vegetables steaming and pecan chicken on the stove. Is that okay with you?" She lifted the lid to check on everything.

"Sounds great." Stad caught a whiff of the vegetables as it mixed in with the aroma of the chicken. "Smells even better."

"Thanks. I'm not much of a cook since I'm usually too busy. Most of the time I just grab a handful of frozen dinners for the week and live off the microwave."

"That's at least probably cheaper than getting fast food like I do almost all the time."

"Might be cheaper but they start to all taste the same after a while."

"I hope you weren't slaving away in the kitchen all day on account of me." Stad tipped his bottle back.

"Oh don't worry about it. This meal's not that hard to make."

"Good," Stad said. "I'm not used to having anyone cook for me, or do much of anything for me really. So thanks again."

"No problem. I've known for a long time that you were more of 'lone wolf' guy anyway."

"How long are we talking here?" Stad tried to figure out if they had already had this conversation or one close enough to it for her to figure it out.

"Pretty much since I first met you."

"How?"

"For starters, I first met you when you were in a bar by yourself and you mentioned that you knew the bartender really well, that was the first clue. Then you talked about how much your work life consumes you and that you can be called away on such sort noticed and I figured you were a workaholic, and every workaholic I've known has not had many close relationships." She took the chicken off the stove.

"Okay, you've got me on the bar thing, but for the work stuff I could use the same argument against you. What about all those weekends you work and the weird hours you're running around?"

"I'm not trying to offend you. It's just who you are and I'm obviously okay with who that person is." She smiled.

Stads guilt kicked into high gear. How could he stare at her and pretend like he was a person he wasn't? It was torture for him to let her go on thinking like nothing was wrong. He wanted to spill everything to her and tell her the real person he was, but the timing wasn't right yet.

"I know," he said instead. "I've just been burned by all types of relationships before and started to find that it just wasn't worth trying to develop any others."

"So what's different about me?" Nikki asked.

"Everything."

Stad could see Nikki move her lips but he didn't hear her words or respond. He was lost in his own thoughts about what made that statement true and the pressure to tell her everything mounted. He couldn't decide what to do. His mind raced ahead of the consequences and the aftermath and focused on his life after the job. He was wrapped up in his dilemma. He knew he had to get it off his chest.

"Stad?" Nikki's voice finally broke through.

"Sorry, I've had a lot running through my head lately."

"Work stuff?"

"Mostly."

"Want to talk about it over a delicious meal?"

"Yeah, I think that'd be good. Maybe it'll let me get some decent sleep tonight." Stad got up from the stool and headed over to the kitchen. He picked up some plates and walked them over to the dining room. Nikki followed behind with a half-empty beer bottle and her own glass of wine.

"Thanks again," Stad said, taking a seat. "I wish I could have done more to help."

"All you had to do was show up." Nikki took her knife and sliced her chicken breast down the middle. She cut off a smaller piece and stabbed it with her fork. "So tell me, what's been bothering you?"

Everything.

Stad wanted to tell her but it was hard just thinking of something to say after so many years of suppressing it. He didn't even know where to begin. He stared down at his dead chicken and took a gulp of his beer. Flashes of conversations with Max and his supplier sped through his mind. He searched for a starting point, something, anything that he could offer to Nikki. At least something was better than nothing, which was what he had now. He looked up from his meat and saw her staring back, chewing her own meal like she had been starved in solitary confinement. She was waiting for any kind of information, something else to sink her teeth into. This was the point where she wanted answers and once again, Stad didn't have any. She wanted to know more, hear more, anything, something that would make her stand out from all the others. She just needed something to latch onto.

He knew she was beginning to worry, maybe wondering if she had pried too much and taken the armor off before the warrior was ready. She was concentrating on her meat, but he was sure his silence was eating her up inside. All she wanted were a few words and instead she just had to stare across the table at him. His mind stopped sorting the memories. There was nothing useful to talk on as nothing in the past would make sense to anyone else. He reverted to an instinct that he had long ago become so good at repressing that it no longer felt natural. He was going to tell her the truth.

"Nikki…" He slowed his pace so as not to get ahead of himself. He needed to be delicate but clear. He had to be precise. He struggled to form words and imagined thoughts running through Nikki's head like "Nikki, I don't want to be with you anymore," or "Nikki, I've been cheating on you," or "Nikki, I have cancer and am only expected to live until tomorrow," or if he was lucky enough she was thinking "Nikki, I love you." He knew the truth would be far harder to accept.

"Nikki, I haven't been completely truthful with you."

She stopped chewing and swallowed whatever was left before placing her fork back down on her plate. "About what?"

"My job, mostly." He paused. "I don't really have any other path than to be direct with you so I'll just tell you. I'm not an accountant."

"Okay." She kept staring at him, egging him to go on. He could only imagine that she was now cycling through worst-case scenarios.

"I don't even do anything remotely related to accounting. I couldn't even tell you what an accountant does."

"I get it, Stad." She became more annoyed with each syllable. "What do you do?"

"I work for a firm that sabotages companies."

"Like a spy stealing secrets?"

"Not exactly. I guess you could say that we're more aggressive. I can't really give you details because the job description changes on a regular basis."

"Okay, can you give me an example?"

"Remember that house you were trying to sell that had that mailbox that blew up?"

"Yes…" She trailed off. He was sure she knew where it was headed but wasn't surprised that the shock stopped her from saying anything else.

"Well that whole thing was engineered by the company I work for. We were hired by delivery companies who wanted us to turn people against using regular mail and switch to deliveries." Nikki was staring blankly back at him so he decided to throw another example at her. "Or you know those recent issues with cars acting strange and the drivers losing control? That was us too. We planted lots of complaints, spread it out into the media and let the public do the rest."

"What? Are you serious right now or are you just making this up?" Nikki's face was turning red and Stad couldn't tell if she was getting really upset or trying to hold back laughter.

"I am completely serious."

"So how are you involved? Where do you fit in? Are you in the back office doing paperwork or something?"

"Not exactly." Stad took a deep breath. "I'm the one doing most of the stuff."

"What? But that's terrible. You do terrible things for a living. Those bombs you put out there could have killed someone." Nikki jumped off her coiled springboard and threw her hands up every time the word "terrible" came out of her mouth. She was waiting for this moment all along and Stad had no defense but to be straightforward.

"We try to take every precaution to make sure no one is seriously harmed."

"Seriously harmed? So you're okay with just being maimed? You couldn't have possibly had any control over those bombs."

"I did." Stad jumped back in to try and take control. "I did tons of research about timing, who was going to be around, tons of stuff. I'm not just going out there and blowing things up randomly. You might not like what I do but I do it in a professional way."

"How can you call risking the lives of hundreds of people professional in any sense of the word? And I can only assume all of your traveling has just been a cover too, right? Are you flying around the country blowing shit up all over the place?" Nikki stood up and started pacing behind her chair. Stad stood too so he wasn't overmatched.

"Some of those weren't me. Some were copycat incidents that we have no control over."

"But some were you?"

"Some were, yes."

"Unbelievable. And you know people will copy you and you know you can't control them and you know that someone's life is in danger? And you're okay with that? How can you live with stuff like that on your conscious? You're manipulating people into thinking these are things that are okay to do."

"That's bull." Stad raised his voice. "You know as well as I do that people can make up their own damn minds. I'm not forcing them to blow up anything or do anything else."

"Does this have anything to do with what you showed me about the warning labels? Are you trying to recruit me?"

"No."

"Or trying to get me to do your dirty work for you?"

"No, that's not related at all. Besides, I've stopped now because you made me realize how much of a terrible person I was for doing it."

"But you're okay with your job? Doesn't that sound ridiculous to you? If anything I'd rather have you quit your job than stop writing over stupid labels. How does one make sense to you and the other doesn't?"

"That's kind of what I wanted to talk about actually."

"You want to talk about something? What is there to talk about? I don't even know if I can look at you let alone have a civil discussion. Give me one good reason I shouldn't kick you out of here or call the cops right now."

"Okay, I know you're upset."

"What gave it away?"

"And I know you want to kick me out, but I just need to tell you that the feelings I have for you and everything we've shared is very much real and true. I haven't lied to you about any of that."

"Kind of hard to trust you now, isn't it?"

"Absolutely, and I can understand if you don't want to have anything to do with me anymore. I just need you to know that I'm sharing this with you for a reason. I trust you more than anyone I have ever been able to before and I think you feel the same way too, at least before tonight." Stad saw Nikki begin to calm down, so he continued on. "And while you may not feel that what I do is moral or right or whatever, I had to tell you because I don't know what to do anymore and you're the only person I can trust in helping me through this." He took a deep breath, closed his eyes and hoped for the best. After a moment or two he looked across the table.

"I think of myself as an open-minded person." Nikki sat down. "So I'm willing to hear what you have to say, but I'm not very happy and I can't guarantee that I'll help you or even want to help you at this point."

"I know, but please try your hardest to be that open-minded person."

"I'll try." Nikki folded her arms and kicked one leg up onto her knee.

"If I've seemed somewhat out of it lately it's because I've been distracted by the latest job they want me to do. This one is targeting a huge industry with a lot of swing and the job itself is very risky. Basically what it boils down to is if I do something wrong or screw up or don't do it at all they're going to try their hardest to hunt me down."

"What is it?" Nikki asked. Her tone was cold and icy.

"They want me to make an attack against the movie industry." Stad could see her expression remain the same, so he continued. "They want me to open fire in a movie theater."

"You're not going to do it, are you?" Nikki's voice was louder and her face was starting to turn red again.

"I told my boss I would think about it."

"Think about it? Think about what? What do you possibly have to think about? The answer has to be no. There's absolutely no way you can go through with something like that. That's just absurd."

"I don't think I want to, but I feel like I have to." Stad started speaking with his hands and grasped the air in front of him. "Let me explain-"

"There's nothing to explain, just tell him you can't, just say no."

"I can't, it's not that easy."

"It's very easy. No, no, no. See?"

"If I say no there are just consequences that I'm not ready to deal with. Besides, I've already done research-"

"Research? What the hell does that mean? I can't believe you're thinking of going through with it."

"It's nothing, I just make sure the plan will be successful and try to minimize the risks."

"So what, you go to the movies and play it out in your head?" Nikki sat there and watched Stad say nothing, which was a dead giveaway. "Oh my God, I can't believe you'd do that. Did you see the innocent and helpless people you'd be slaughtering while you were at it? Was our date to the movies just a cover to get some work done? You're unbelievable, you're a monster." She stood up. "I don't think I want you here anymore, you disgust me."

"The date had nothing to do with my job." Stad stood up to take a stronger stance. "Listen, I'm not dragging you into this mess with me, it's just something I have to deal with and was hoping you'd be able to help me because I don't know what to do."

"Help you with what? I don't see any possible reason you'd actually do this, it just doesn't make any sense. The only thing you can do is not go through with it."

"I told you, there are serious consequences. If I don't do this then our client is going to come after my boss, me and if they know about you, you'd be on their list to. I can't have anything happen to you and I don't know what horrible things they'd do, but I do know I don't want to find out. If all I have to do is put a few strangers in harm's way to protect the ones closest to me, I'll make that trade every day."

"But all you're doing is trading in certain harm to others for possible harm to us, to me. I don't think that's fair."

"I never thought I'd be saying this but you're something I've never had before and it's something I don't want to lose."

"You can't assume the worst. Are your clients really going to risk exposing themselves just to get revenge on someone they don't even know?"

"I don't know, I just couldn't imagine anything happening to you."

"It's admirable, but I don't want to be involved in it, Stad. You just have to promise me that you're not going to go through with this. You said you'd be broken if anything happened to me, and I'm telling you that I'd be broken if I saw you go through with this. I'm not sure if I still want to be with you or not, but I can guarantee that if you go through with this, we're done. I couldn't imagine being with a person who not only does those terrible things, but continues to do them knowing they disappoint me. I just don't think I could do that."

"I just don't know what to do."

"You asked me for help and I gave you the advice I thought you needed to hear. You don't have to take it if you don't want to, but you do have to know where I stand on it and I know that I can't be with someone who would go through with something this atrocious."

"I know, but all I'm trying to do is look out for you and I don't think you understand the dangerous situation I'd put us all in-"

"I don't think you understand. I won't be able to look at you the same way anymore if you do this. I just won't. So unless that's what you want, I suggest you tell your boss to screw off and find someone else."

"I know, but-"

"I don't want to hear it, I really don't. I think I've put up with this long enough. I've been open minded like you asked and I found that hard enough. I think I'm going to need some time to accept who the new Stad is."

"I'm still the same person."

"I can't be around you tonight. I think you need to leave." She walked over to the door and unlocked it.

"You don't want to talk about anything?"

"I think we've done all the talking we can for tonight. I just want some time to think." She opened the door.

"Okay." Stad stood up and started to walk toward Nikki but she backed into the kitchen as he neared the entryway. He grabbed his jacket and turned to face her. "Don't let this be the end."

"I'm just going to need some time."

"Promise me it won't be long." Stad stepped outside.

"I can't promise you anything right now." She closed the door. Stad was left standing alone on her front steps.

50

Stad rambled down the street in his used car toward the storage unit on the old dirt road. He sent messages to both Nikki and Max earlier in the day but only Max had responded. All it said was "Don't let me down." He knew Nikki's reply would be similar.

He pulled up in front of the storage unit, opened it and stepped inside. He saw the gun, silencer and ammo sitting near the empty space on the shelf where the pipe bomb used to be. The light from the bare bulb gleamed off the metal barrel and bounced around the walls of the container. He walked over to the weapon and picked it up. It was heavier than he had expected and the grip was cool. The realness of the situation wrapped around his mind and Nikki's words rattled him again. Stad forced his arm to reach for the silencer and when he screwed it on, the weapon became even heavier.

He aimed at the far blank storage unit wall and the metal faded away and turned into a movie crowd. Everyone was laughing and cheering and oohing and aahing. Nobody noticed him aiming the barrel of a silenced gun at them, but nobody cared. The people were busy throwing popcorn and soda down their throats and staring at the flashing pictures in front of them. Stad forced his finger to squeeze the trigger and the daydream faded away. Back inside the storage unit the click of the tightened trigger echoed off the walls. After the crowd disappeared and the noise died down, there was nothing but silence.

***

He pulled into the parking lot of Sycamore 6 with the gun tucked into his pants. He headed for the box office and noticed that he was weighed down more than he imagined during his practice run. Even with the added weight and assurance that the gun was still with him, he had to keep brushing his hand by and touching it every so often to make sure it hadn't gone anywhere.

One teenager gave him his ticket for "Destined for Death" and another one inside ripped it in two. He headed down the same hallway as before, passing the bathrooms and drinking fountains and the innocent moviegoers. The theater was much more crowded than it had been before and people were squeezing by each other just to walk around. Stad made plenty of room between himself and the others to make sure nobody bumped into the gun or silencer against his legs.

He managed to get past everyone and make his way to the theater. He walked up the stairs to the planned location, took a seat, checked his watch and made sure he knew all of his surroundings before the lights dimmed and it was too dark to see anything. There was still plenty of time before the movie started, about 30 minutes, so Stad watched the crowd pour in. Most of the first wave consisted of families with smaller children, maybe 14 or 15 year olds, mostly boys and a lapful of popcorn, candy and soda. The second wave was the couples. The men were wearing some of their best shirts and carrying around snacks as their dates chose the best seats. The last groups of people to start filling the scattered empty seats were the packs of roaming teenagers. A group of guys here and another over there just showing up to see a lot of action and maybe a little nudity. Stad scanned the crowd again for anything he may have missed.

He had tried to suppress his thoughts and run on adrenaline alone, but Nikki popped into his brain. He didn't want to lose her, especially now that he had let her in closer than anyone else in his life. She was open minded about his situation and caring and helpful, why would he want to lose someone like that? Doubts flooded his mind. He pulled his phone out to see if she had texted anything back, and to his surprise she had. When he pulled up her response all it said was "You know the right thing to do." He looked back at the crowd and the words repeated in his head. He flipped to the next message from Max, "Don't let me down." He looked back up at the crowd and tried to figure out a way to compromise with his thoughts. He couldn't make a decision, he had never struggled like this and now it was the worst possible timing.

The lights dimmed and the trailers started.

51

Stad slipped out of the theater and tried to blend in with the people leaving the horror movie. He tried to focus on their conversations instead of what just happened. He overheard that the twist ending was good and was lucky enough that nobody asked what he thought about it. He limped around the building with the gun still weighing him down and headed for his car.

Cars were lined up trying to get out and Stad weaved in and out of traffic, cutting people off before finally reaching the exit. The light turned yellow and he stomped on the gas and sped through.

All of the logic in Stad's head was telling him to go home and lay low but his instincts won over. He stopped at the mall and parked next to one of the huge anchor department stores. On his way inside he called Nikki. If only he could hear her voice and talk to her things would be much better. His pace picked up with every unanswered ring and after waiting too long, her voicemail finally picked up.

"Nikki, I need to see you. I know you're probably not ready to see me yet but I think it's important that we talk. Please call me when you get this." He slipped his phone back into his pocket and hoped that she would listen to his message and realize that she needed him in her life as much as he needed her.

Once inside the store he didn't make eye contact with anyone yet somehow felt like he was being watched. He passed aisle after aisle and had a nagging feeling that he was being followed. He picked an aisle full of irons and hair dryers to dart into to avoid the internal glare. There was a young woman studying one of the irons like it was the most important purchase of her life and she must have noticed Stad because she peered up from her in-depth research and smiled. He didn't feel like smiling at all but in an attempt to avoid suspicion and appear somewhat stable and normal, he smiled back. He walked past her and pretended like he had chosen the wrong aisle.

The next row over was small appliances. He made sure it was clear before he started scanning boxes for ill-conceived warning labels. It was wrong and he felt sick doing it again, but after what had just happened, it didn't matter anyway. On one of the cheaper brands of coffee makers he spotted a perfect candidate that said, "Warning: Coffee produced may be hot," so he bent over and crossed it out with his black marker.

He was able to cross out two more before an older man walked into the row. Stad transitioned from criminal mischief to curious consumer. He placed his hands on his hips and pretended to be contemplating a purchase. After a couple of seconds he shook his head in dramatic fashion so everyone would see his reaction. He turned to walk away and caught the older man's eye on accident.

"Good day," the man said in an old-fashioned manner.

Stad nodded even though he couldn't disagree more.

52

Stad dumped his latest car faster than a drug dealer on the run and hoofed a good mile back to his escape vehicle. He jammed the key into the ignition and peeled out. He turned off the radio and checked behind every tree and around every turn to make sure he wasn't being followed.

He couldn't get to his apartment fast enough. He pulled up, grabbed a parking spot, tucked the gun back into his pants and jogged to the back entrance. It was an entrance he hadn't used in over a year and was surprised when his key opened the lock. When the freight elevator arrived on his floor, he poked his head out and looked up and down and left and right through the hall to confirm there were no unexpected visitors. He took big strides walking to his door and when he reached it, he crashed through and double checked the lock behind him. He threw the gun in his lock box and tried to forget that he ever had it in his possession.

His phone beeped but he was too busy taking off his clothes to check it. He knew it was Max. He could see his boss pacing around his desk, cursing up and down. He wanted updates and information, but that would have to wait. Stad tossed his sweat-soaked shirt into the corner of the bathroom and took the coldest shower of his life. 30 minutes and half a bar of soap later he decided he needed to head over to the office. With a fresh change of clothes and no gun tugging on his pants, Stad headed down the same elevator and walked the same path to get to his shaded car. He was less nervous in the streets this time but he still looked over his shoulder at every chance he got and stared down the cameras above the stoplights to make sure they weren't secretly recording his every move or logging the coordinates of his vehicle. While waiting at one of the suspicious stops he called Nikki again. After numerous rings her voicemail kicked in.

"It's me again. Look, I know I haven't given you the time you probably wanted or needed, but I really need to see you. It's very important, so when you get this, please call me."

He reached his work building without being followed. He stepped inside, blew past the security guard and took the elevator up, wishing it would move faster through the floors. He stormed out of the elevator and headed for the door at the end of the long hallway. He was expecting to have to bang on it again and hope that Max would let him in, but he turned the last corner and wasn't worried about it anymore. The door swung open and Max stepped out.

53

"This is a disaster!" one of the suits exclaimed from his leathery chair.

"I knew we shouldn't have gone through with this." Another one piped up from across the table.

The expressions and angst hung above the oak table where the cigarette smoke used to be. The man in black, once again at the end of the table, tried to sort it all out. The Three Bald Mice sat in their seats with "smug" written across their shiny foreheads.

"All right, let's just calm down," the man in black projected above all the noise. "We don't know all the facts yet."

"We don't need to know all the facts, what about that leak on the news? It doesn't matter what happened, we're already ruined."

"We're not ruined." The man in black had already consumed his glass of water and it sat empty on the coaster. The female assistant was not there to get a refill for him.

"We have to go after him, he lied all the way to the bank," another anonymous suit shouted.

"Now wait a minute, we haven't even paid them yet, don't worry about that," the man in black said.

"Well then maybe they need to pay us for all these damages we have to try and smooth out. How the hell are we supposed to do that?"

"We've got people on the phone trying to get in touch with them to figure out what's going on. In the meantime we'll have to deploy a full blown PR assault." The man in black scratched his face and his hand continued up to his scalp where it smoothed out his already smoothed out hair.

"We need action, we don't need any more plans."

"Yeah," another suit agreed with the first. "The last time we had plans they blew up in our faces. We need to go after them, we need to hit them hard and hit them right now before they can get away with or leak anything else."

"Let's fight back, get ahead of the rumors. We need to stamp out this fire." The voices were blending together now and the man in black tilted his head back and stared at the ceiling. Everyone was in a flurry over the outcome and it didn't look good for him or anyone else in the room. The suits gestured with their hands and turned in their chairs and were getting riled up. The man in black tried to block it all out. Suit #1 would not want to hear about this.

54

"What the fuck, Stad?" Max slammed the door the second Stad got far enough inside.

"I can't do this anymore. I want out," Stad said, turning to meet his boss' stare.

"No shit you can't do this anymore, you can't even do one simple job." Max walked over to his desk.

"Simple job? It wasn't just a simple job. And you'd know that if you weren't too busy wheeling and dealing out there with other clients offering them shit you know we don't have the capacity for. Don't tell me it's just a simple job."

"I'll tell you what I damn feel like telling you. You still work for me." Max thumped his chest for emphasis. "And I work for the clients, and they're not too happy right now."

"Do they need a reason why I didn't go into that movie today and kill a bunch of innocent people? Do they have serious questions behind my motive? What's their motive?"

"We don't question their intentions, we act. That trickles down from them, to me, to you. But no, they don't care nearly as much about that as they do what's been scrolling across the headlines today. Rumors are circulating about a plot to attack a movie theater with a plan that was just a little too familiar."

Shit. Stad couldn't believe this. Did he trust his supplier enough? Maybe the reason he moved around so much was because he kept backstabbing the people who hired him. But that didn't make any sense, the two of them didn't have much contact about this job anyway. How long ago did he tell him? Was that even enough time to spread any rumors?

"We haven't been able to track down where the rumors started," Max continued, "but they're already spiraling out of control, pointing fingers at terrorists, extremists and one suspect that isn't much of a rumor at all..."

"The home entertainment industry." The words fell out of Stad's mouth.

"Exactly, and big surprise, they're not too happy about it. They're hounding me for answers and calling for my head, not to mention they're also telling us that they'd give us up in a heartbeat saying that if the shit hits the fan, it's going to land in our lap. They're already demanding compensation." Max sat down. "Like I said earlier, it all trickles down Stad and unfortunately, you're at the bottom. I can only protect you so much, but I'm sure they'll be coming after you too."

"Why can't they just shrug it off as a false rumor and cut their losses?" Stad asked.

"That's not how they like to play the game. They claw and fight and scratch their way out of things until all that's left is a bloody mess of a skeleton and then they keep on fighting. If they do go down, we're going with them. Maybe if we can find the source of this rumor we can pin it on them. Now we know someone leaked, and the only people I know who have been involved are me, you and your contact."

"My supplier wouldn't spill anything, he doesn't have any reason to, that doesn't make sense. We've been working fine together for years."

"Well Stad." Max leaned forward. "I know it wasn't me, so if what you're saying is true and your contact didn't leak, that only leaves us with one person. I don't think you're trying to tell me you undermined your own work."

"None of this makes any sense." Stad stumbled back. "How could this have possibly leaked?"

"I don't know Stad, but you better start looking into it because that undercover maintenance worker at the water bottling plant was arrested today too."

"That has to be my supplier, he was the only one who had contact with the insider."

"All I've heard is that an anonymous tip led the police to him and they found some extra tainted caps in his possession," Max said. "From what I can tell he hasn't given anyone up yet, but we all know that can only last for so long. I can almost guarantee you they'll get something out of him and we'll be discovered."

Max's words jumped into Stad's head and pummeled his brain. Since he first started here he thought about this day, the day their cover was blown, the day the entire operation was over. He thought it was going to happen after the exploding battery job, he hadn't done a great job covering his tracks on that one. A few weeks passed and nothing came of it, then those weeks turned into months and then into years and he had forgotten about it. The same thing happened with the poisoned spinach. After both of those he was sure the gig was up and had prepared for it, he had plane tickets and everything, but this time he was caught off guard. Maybe the chemical manufacturer got suspicious or maybe his supplier couldn't take it anymore and had enough money and wanted out. Whatever it was Stad knew he would be facing it soon enough.

"Shit." Stad placed his hands on his hips and bent forward at the waist to try and get some deeper breathes. His knees wiggled back and forth. "So what are we supposed to do?"

"The only thing we can do, burn as much evidence as we can, relocate and start over. You in?"

"Honestly Max, I came here today hoping that I'd never have to return, but this isn't really what I had in mind."

"Look, I know it's not ideal, but we're not completely screwed yet. By the time they're onto our scent we'll have a new one. This isn't the worst thing that could have happened, I mean it's up there, but it could be worse."

"Sorry Max, I have to give it up. Maybe last year I would have thought about it, had some more fight, but I'm done."

"Suit yourself." Max stood up and walked over to his filing cabinets. "I'm going to get busy burning everything and I suggest you do the same. Get out of your apartment too, find a new state if you have too. Hell, maybe even a new country. I'm just hoping our paths will cross again."

Stad didn't respond, he didn't have anything to say. Instead, he stood up and started walking for the door.

"If I never see you again," Max said, "good luck."

55

Stad headed back down the hall and punched the button for the elevator. He opened his phone to see if he had any missed calls or messages from Nikki but nothing popped up on the status bar. He called her again, but when no one answered he didn't leave a message.

The events that just unfolded were bouncing around in his skull. Walking outside and heading for his car only made the thoughts grow louder and more intense. He tried focusing on other things like the sidewalk, the sky, that guy across the street, but all that he could hear were terrible thoughts.

Was this really how it was going to end?

His whole career, what he had built his life on all gone in what seemed to be a five-second dream. He raced across the street, jumped in his car and slammed the door hoping it would leave all the noise and thoughts blocked out. He turned the ignition and the thoughts came back to life along with the engine.

He knew that logic should win, but he found his instincts taking over once again and headed for another department store. He was no longer worried about the spying cameras above the stoplights or even laying low as he sped through the streets. Once the store appeared in the distance he stepped harder on the gas and took a shot at the parking lot.

He screeched to a halt and was up and out of his car and walking to the front entrance before the engine had stopped making noises. The automatic doors flung themselves open and he was greeted with a blast of fresh air. The flooring looked familiar and the lighting above was bringing back old memories. The way the stored smelled like old plastic and cleaning supplies and the way the employees shuffled around and put on fake characters made him feel like he had been in the same place sometime in the past.

The memories stopped and the thoughts of pure terror began to take over again. He picked up his pace to get to the home maintenance section. He did a quick up and down investigation of the aisle, cruising past hand saws and drills and screwdrivers and safety goggles before finding some boxes of nails. He grabbed the first box he saw and on the back, in the smallest print possible saw the words "Harmful if swallowed."

He pulled a familiar marker from his pocket and dragged it across the warning, making the words null and void to anyone who was concerned. He started feeling guilty again and could only imagine how upset Nikki would be if she was here, but she wasn't. He wasn't sure she would ever be around again. She hadn't called him back, sent him any messages or indicated that she cared about him at all. He had to find out why. She was the one who wanted this in the first place, she was the one who wanted more commitment and a sense of direction so why was she the one cutting off communication now? If he was never going to see her again he had to get a reason. He was the one who needed answers now. He left the store and the terrible thoughts and cruel images banging around in his head became muted.

56

Stad stepped back out into the miserable heat and walked through the parking lot. His head was still telling him that he had to do everything he could to make sure he destroyed all evidence and any traces of his existence, but he was running on adrenaline now and his overwhelming feelings had taken over. He jumped back in his car and headed for Nikki's apartment.

He couldn't understand why she had not gotten back to him. There was the possibility that she didn't want to talk to him, but he thought that she would have realized how important it was after his fourth call.

He turned left onto Elmhurst and worst case scenarios ran through his mind. What if she really didn't want to have anything to do with him anymore? Maybe she moved away and pulled a stunt that he was about to. Maybe she beat him to the punch and burned all of her evidence and moved out of state. He didn't want to think it a possibility but he had to at least consider it. He had sacrificed his career and life to protect her and she didn't even know. He had to tell her to get her back in his life. He weaved back and forth on the roads and the thoughts of her not being around started to mix with everything else and the noise became a huge distraction.

Off in the distance he could make out a "Parkview Place" sign and when he reached it he turned into the lot and headed around back. He parked in the same spot as last time and jumped out. He ran across the parking lot and tried to think of what he would say to her. He hoped he wasn't making things worse by showing up at her door unannounced. He considered turning around and going home but instead stopped at the bottom of the stairs and calculated his moves. If he went up there he would risk pissing her off even more or driving her away if he hadn't already done that. If he didn't go up there and see her today there was a good chance he would never see her again. If she hadn't made up her mind already then he knew he'd be gone by the time she did. He knew he had to take the chance, so with a deep breath he started to climb the stairs.

He reached the top after second-guessing himself all the way up and walked the agonizing path to her front step. Without hesitation he knocked and waited.

He knew this was the right thing to do and no longer needed to consider anything. He had to give her explanations and it had to be done today or it would languish for eternity and she would be the one that got away. He had pushed people away his whole life and was tired of it. He finally had someone that was right and he couldn't let go.

He knocked again and kept waiting.

If she was inside and still angry with him he figured it would at least be common courtesy to come to the door and tell him. A simple "I don't want to talk" would do, or even opening the chain and letting him see her face and catch a hint of her strawberry perfume.

He knocked for a third time and started to get impatient.

"Nikki," he said through the door. "I don't know exactly how you're feeling now, and I'm sorry if I've made you upset coming over like this, but I didn't have a choice. I have to see you today. If you can hear me please open the door." He let a couple minutes of complete silence pass. After getting no indication of life inside, he grabbed the handle and turned. He didn't expect anything to happen but the handle kept moving. The door gave way and he pushed until it was open just enough for him to step into Nikki's apartment.

"Hello?" He stopped with one foot still outside and the other on the tile of the entryway. He waited and gave her a chance to respond. When nothing returned his call, he stepped all the way inside and shut the door. He stood frozen and listened for any noise. He looked around for something but he wasn't sure what. All he noticed was that there weren't any dishes on the counter, or papers on the couch, or shoes by the door. There was just a bunch of empty space, just like it had always been.

"Hello?" he called out again, a little louder this time. He walked into the living room, then the hallway. The doors to every room were open and all he could see in the bedroom was her dresser and a messy bed. The scent of her strawberry perfume still lingered in the air. He grabbed the door frame to her bedroom and swung his upper body in to turn on the lights. He confirmed there was nothing else in there but a bed and dresser.

"Nikki?" Nobody answered. He flipped the lights off and kept walking. He made his way to the office and turned on the lights. There was a lamp on the desk and it lit up the surface that was covered in papers and documents.

"Anyone here?" he yelled again and started to step toward the desk. He got closer and the documents laid out got clearer and he could start making out words.

His heart almost stopped. He couldn't breathe. Panic kicked in and the horrendous thoughts poured back into his head like a tidal wave.

He reached down and grabbed a handful of papers, shuffling through them with every muscle that could help. There was a report on the bottled water job and a copy of Max's presentation to the industry. There were duplicates of the memos and reports he had dug up about all of the companies involved. He tossed those over his shoulder and revealed the next layer that had his research notes for both the movie job and the bottled water job. There was even a detailed diagram of the capsules that he and his supplier had come up with and they were stapled together with emails between the two of them. There were binders full of information on all of his research for the movie job and profiles of the industry players from the home entertainment industry who ordered the action, something not even Stad had access to.

He flung the reports aside and revealed more details. A picture of his supplier was staring back at him along with information on the location he operated out of as well as his own contacts, including the insider at the bottling plant. There were blueprints and detailed specification sheets for all of the buildings he used and reports on how he got all of his supplies.

Stad threw those to the ground and then found his flight plan and schedule for his trip to Atlanta as well as details on Max's office, paper clipped to pictures of both Stad and Max leaving and entering the building. He threw those to the floor and they landed with the thud of a lifetime on top of the other incriminating papers.

This was it. This was the end.

Stad turned around and sat on the corner of the desk. His head dropped and he stared at the papers on the ground. He dangled there, helpless. He had been used, just like he had used so many before. He went from being at the top of his game to the bottom of everyone else's. The competition was catching up. It was a complete turnaround and Stad didn't know what to do in an unfamiliar position. He knew he should have called Max and told him that it was all over, that the one person he thought he could trust had been the total opposite. He knew he should tell his boss that police would be storming his office in no time. He knew that he himself should get out of the apartment and drive. He didn't know where he should go, but he knew he just needed to drive, just get out of town. He knew he had to do something, but he couldn't bring himself to do anything. His logic and instincts had run out, and like his body they had given up.

He was relieved.

It was a type of freedom that he never expected or had ever experienced before, but it was nice. He sat on the edge of the desk and didn't think about his career, he didn't think about his company, he didn't think about the lives he had impacted over the years and he didn't think about Nikki and how she had manipulated him. He was done thinking about it all. He didn't think about anything.

He didn't even flinch when the officers waltzed through the door with their guns drawn and manhandled him to the ground. He had given up already anyway. He was put in handcuffs, read his rights and hauled out, but he didn't care anymore. He smiled the whole time.

www.ingramcontent.com/pod-product-compliance
Lightning Source LLC
Chambersburg PA
CBHW050932120626
46552CB00001B/167